ALLU

Valos of Son

by Ama

Cover Art by Cameron Kamenicky
Edited by the awesome LY Services and the talented Tiffany Roberts *(Along with a brick-ton of other generous souls who also gave up their hours and families to help a book out. (Dawn, Cindy, Lyda, Linda, Ronika, Yui, Christine, you rock ♥) I am grateful beyond measure, and you are freaking fantastic.)*
...And when you find errors despite all of the fabulous assistance, the blame definitely can't be laid on them; know that they TRIED. ;D

1

Dedicated to R.
(Psst! Thanks for all the times you calmed that crazy Yasai while I worked!)

What the heck am I reading?

Right, so you're probably wondering why this doesn't look like the *Stolen, Rescued, Won* universe.

That's because... it isn't.

Don't yell!

I haven't forgotten: I just took a side-trip. I was invited to write with eight other scifi and fantasy romance authors. Each one of us wrote a standalone story, and they're designed to be read in any order, but we've woven little 'easter eggs' and plot details into each other's books for a richer experience should you decide to tackle the entire series.

Each one ends with a Happily Ever After.

If we did it right, you'll wish you had an alien (or two, or ten) of your very own by the time you're done. (A few stories are Reverse Harem, some are Ménage, and one is a traditional couple of two. This book, *Alluvial*, is a Reverse Harem, and will be the last RH I release until after Dohrein and Gracie [then Crispin and Laura] have their stories told.)

Happy reading! =)

ALIEN NAME SUGGESTIONS,
Dictionaries, and Drunk Birds:

YOU'VE BEEN ASKING me to make dictionaries, and I'm going to work on that retroactively, but this time—check this out!—I got one done *before* it was published.

I know. I'm shocked too!

But that's not all this is. I love weird and random factoids. My research for this story? Ant sex and Amazon penis trees.

I freaking love the job you've given me.

THANK YOU for supporting my weird-facts-collecting habit! Some of you have even joined in =D

The following are real words, with no changes to make them 'alien':

Alluvial: rich, fertile soil

Scion: a living bud or shoot that is grafted onto an established living plant

Caber: a large, thick log

Prevernal: [of plants] early flowering and unfolding their leaves or petals

Bole: a tree's trunk

Tarn: a mountain lake, formed by a glacier

Now for a book Dictionary/Factoid-Inspiry tidbits breakdown:

Sonhadra: A planet inhabited by alien lifeforms, including several sentient races, located far, far from Earth.

The *Concord:* An orbital prison ship that is sectioned into pods—Alphapod, Betapod, and so on. The overall formation is flower-like, with each pod having a petal shape.

IPS: Interstellar Penitentiary System

Valos: a race either native to Sonhadra, or created there

Valos Element: Earth

Heroine name: Preta, taken from *Terra preta* (literally "black soil" in Portuguese) is a type of very fertile soil found in the Amazon Basin.

FUN FACTOID: According to some folk religions, Preta is a supernatural being that undergoes suffering greater than that of humans, particularly an extreme level of hunger and thirst.

Sol: Latin for sun, also Spanish for sun *[Poppy Rhys gets full credit for this! She's brilliant at backstory and chose this as the sisters' last name.]*

Cattleya Orchid: Grown in Brazil, the green, yellow, and brown-spotted species *(Brassocattleya Hippodamia)* inspired the eyes of the heroes.

'Amazon Penis Trees': Photos of these trees inspired some... features.

***Hormiga culona* Ants:** These ants from the Amazon are believed to be aphrodisiacs.

[Before you send me all the notes, I didn't say I believe it to be true, I'm wiki-facting you on what the natives believe, and Artistic Licensing the crap out of it because it inspired a crazy-fun plot.]

Ants are Strong: Despite their tiny size, they can easily lift far more than their own body weight.

Drunk Hummingbirds: If you feed hummingbirds, you probably already know this—hummingbirds can get drunk on nectar. This happens when nectar has fermented. In this story, the substance isn't fermented, it isn't harmful, and the reaction happens when there is a great excess of pollen. *Yep, I'm pulling the Artistic License Card again: Go with it, just go with it.* ;D

The Rocks are REAL: The multicolored rocks described in the tarn in this story are not fiction! The Pebbles of Montana's Lake McDonald in Glacier National park are worth a Google image search—unless you can visit, in which case, WOW, have a great time! It looks *incredible*.

ALIEN NAME SUGGESTIONS:

On the Amanda Milo's Minions Facebook group, I asked for name suggestions, preferably with a significance to soil.

You'll find the following name ideas were used in various ways all over this story.

It was so fun to do. THANK YOU for playing with me! =D

Neron: Spanish name meaning 'strong' - Lex Hampton

Azibo: Egyptian for "earth" - Eve Steward

Vejo-kaolin: combination of Andy Currey's suggestion of vejo = the initials of her children (♥!) and Lee Allen was Kimber's Kaolin = to do with clay

Salachar: The Irish word for dirt is Salachar. Sounds a bit elfin - Katherine Burger Eftink

Gaius: Yvette Ward Turner

Kor: Nadia Lynn Lambert suggested Kor, and I loved the sound of it so much that Petrichor, which Kate Botting suggested, goes by the nickname of Chor. Love it!

Maceous: as in diatomaceous - Isabel Wroth

Loess: face of the earth - Cyndi Mathewson (When I asked how she would like her name to appear, this is what I got: "CYNDI MATHEWSON, loyal fan of Amanda Milo, is how I would like to be referenced!" *HUGS* You got it! And man. Ha ha ha! I'm still cracking up! ;D)

Devon: Tracy Herzog

Geoss: Laurie Christensen

Petrichor: is the earthy scent produced when rain falls on dry soil. The word is constructed from Greek πέτρα petra, meaning "stone," and ἰχώρ īchōr, the fluid that flows in the veins of the gods in Greek mythology - Kate Botting

Marl: type of clay - Alyssa Higley Fogg

Bort: Bort is considered to be diamond without value so it's used in technical equipment - Sanda Šantare Ābele

Ammos: in Greek in means sand - Andrie Michael

(Just a random note from me [what isn't, right? =D] that Bortammos sounds like Aramis from Three Musketeers to me and it makes me smile every time I say it in my head. ♥)

Caedon: Jean Aldredge

Terran: Linda Bacerra

Zemerac: Combination formed by Sanda Šantare Ābele's suggestion of Zeme who said, in Latvian, Earth and dirt is "Zeme" (capital Z for Earth and regular z for dirt) and Erac by Ronika Williams (also grabbed Mehyam!)

Nitesh: heartbeat of the earth - Sue Handshoe Bec

Granith: Susan Graham

Micha: like mica minerals - Courtney Pinelli

Dikar: Kaila Brieann

Prakrti: Sanskrit for "nature" - Sara Gray Evans

Adarian: Amor Pagsanjan

Sereth: Laura Davis

Ryekeil: Frenda Williams

Throckmorton: Kym Durham

K'Baan: Susan Deahl

Yui Phitchaya Monsintorn: "The word soil in my language [Thai] is 'din,' or if you want a more sophisticated word it's 'pasutha,' so some male will have Pasutha as his formal name and Din for his nickname."

Combined Susan Deahl, Kym Durham, Yui's and Frenda's suggestions to make **Keilmort'baan din,** which in these aliens' tongue means, *'You are welcome.'*

Mustang or Charger?

I knew this story would have an old car in it. This book is set in the future, so this would be a *very* old car, but of all the decisions that needed to be made, it really boiled down to the big one: Mustang or Charger? Thankfully, *I* did not have to make this harrowing call. I let readers decide. =D

CHAPTER 1

PRETA

"FRIGGIN' LEAFCUTTER ants," Drogan pretends to complain as he unzips my suit.

One of the species being used in the project is *hormiga culona*. Little gifts from the Amazon—delicacies consumed for their high protein, and prized for their incredibly potent aphrodisiac qualities.

The research team is doing a little more than feeding me liquefied ants, but I blame the *culonas* for a lot of things.

"Worst job ever?" I ask as he helps me out of my sleeves. I keep my undershirt on, even though Drogan's eyes always seem drawn to my chest. Today is no different; he looks at my cloth-covered boobs mournfully enough that I have to resist the urge to shove my face into his shoulder and guffaw.

It's not that I need assistance getting undressed; it's that he knows I need sex *right now*, and he's doing everything he can to make sure we take advantage of our incredibly small window of opportunity.

He jerks down my stunning atomic-orange jumpsuit, shoving it around my thighs. "Mmm," his hand drops to his fly, and the *zzzziiip!* of metal over metal teeth is getting my pulse racing even faster. "I wouldn't go that far, Preta Sol." His lips quirk up on one side, and it's sexy, and kind of sweet, and it concerns me a little—how much I like his face.

Him. I like him.

Drogan's got the classic good looks with the piercing, jade-green eyes, the high, prominent cheekbones, and the ridiculously thick bottom lip I'd previously thought belonged only to movie stars and models. His looks are enough to make him trouble. His *endearing* streak is the surprise—a disastrous one. It's a complication. *He* is a complication. I squint at him and put my hands on his shoulders. "Less smiling, more sex, please. Time limit, remember? I distinctly remember that I already begged you to tear all my clothes off."

"Work, work, work," he says, quoting one of my favorite old shows as he pretends to take off his uniform.

That's right. His uniform.

Drogan is a guard.

I'm a prisoner.

This is the Alpha pod section of the *Concord,* an orbital prison ship, and he's only joking about the uniform because we don't actually have time for him to undress.

My shoulders hit the wall, his hand grips my ass, and my leg climbs to his hip like this is a dance routine we've done, oh, *three hundred times in approximately one hundred and sixty-five days.*

That first slide into me? *Uunnfff.*

Yet... no magic.

"Higher?" he asks before he hooks my knee over his arm. This angle change is nice, but I'm riding on the edge and can't make it over, and if I don't come soon I feel like I'll *die.*

"Here," his voice is strained and husky as he pulls out, and drops his arm so the back of my orange-clad leg slides down his—former-ly—crisply-pressed black sleeve before he turns me so that I face the wall.

I stifle a moan as he thrusts back in, and his hand wraps around my throat, his thumb clamping under my ear, his fingertip digging into my chin, his grip keeping me locked in place.

I'm frustrated, still not getting there, when his other hand spears into my hair and pulls my head back.

Startled, I try to stand up, but he tugs the fist holding my hair firm-ly, until my head drops back enough that my eyes meet his and—

He kisses me.

Not on the lips—my *forehead*. He doesn't let our eye contact waver, either—his intense greens staring into my bewildered browns, and it's oddly *tender,* and foreign, and it's such a shock to my system that my core gives a delicious clench.

It sets off the world's most pleasurable implosion.

He growls and releases my hair so that he can drop his hand to my waist and use the leverage to piston into me until he comes too.

I'm still floating down from the orgasm high and trying to process what just happened when he curses and swipes a nanocloth between my legs for the world's quickest clean up.

That's right: no condom for a mess-less encounter. This is a prison in *space.* Supplies do get up here, but they go to the people with rank.

Drogan's the new guy, a spot so far down the totem pole he's really only a step ahead of a prisoner in the hierarchy here. At first, he was able to beg, borrow, and pay exorbitant prices to get condoms, but we ran out of the supply in no time.

His lips hit the side of my face, pressing right over my dark, curly flyaway tendrils—in effect, gluing them to my sweat-sticky skin. "No time for round two. Sorry, babe."

I groan, and he squeezes my hip in commiseration. His voice is softer than I expect when he asks, "Gonna make it, Sol?" His tone says, *hold on.*

I don't have a choice: the camera is going to sweep back in our direction, and this corridor is about to lose its blind spot.

He chivalrously assists in setting me to rights before he's dragging me alongside him. My eyes scan him, from his dark hair—the 'could-be-dirty-blond-might-be-brown' buzzfuzz he keeps it at—to the way his uniform stretches across his muscles. Mmm*mm.*

I'm in the middle of ogling how *Concord*-issued clothing somehow does all the right things for his chest, so I do see his arm come towards my face, but I twitch when I feel a teasing flick against my neck; this I was not expecting.

My gaze shoots up to his to see he's smirking at me, and he looks... it isn't a cocky 'bitches-find-me-sexy' expression that he's wearing. It's a playful, fond look. It's a... it's a *dangerous* look, because while Drogan does nice things like conscientiously thinking of post-coital cleanup (which is super nice considering I don't have access to washcloths without permission at predetermined times), and sneaks me the special Icelandic-style yogurts from the guard breakroom, and *kisses* my *forehead,* acting like—treating this... couple-y. Like we-have-a-*future*-y.

My breath rasps out as I revisit the horrifying realization I was struck with weeks ago: *THE RESEARCH TEAM KNOWS.*

By now, they *have* to know. The doctors and lab techs do not strike me as incompetent; they can't have missed the fact that I'm pregnant. My case for this theory? They haven't performed surgeries on me in weeks. It can't be a coincidence. Sometimes, as they stick the monitoring nodes to me, and everyone can hear—everyone can see—my heartrate jackhammering from the fear, I want to shout at them, 'Just SAY it!' *But* if they *don't* know, I'm certainly not going to enlighten them.

If they *don't* know, then the longer I can keep quiet, and survive, the more time it gives my family to assemble a rescue mission.

Whenever I lie awake at night, thoughts chasing each other around and around like a coyote broke into my sleep-sheep's pen and is running them down hard, I keep returning to the fact that I have an implant to prevent fertility. I'm *still* shaking my head in disbelief at our situation. Maybe the chemical cocktails they've been pouring into me overrode a hormone or something.

But wouldn't the team have expected that?

Did they think I'd stay celibate? After the *leafcutter* treatments? Orgasm-denying sadists!

I don't know, and it doesn't exactly matter—the knowledge of *how* doesn't do us a damn bit of good. Drogan must have suspected this possibility though. Or perhaps it was simple male-who-rides-bareback paranoia that drove him to take over the assignment of passing out feminine hygiene products, and start paying special attention to my usage needs—specifically, when I had a lack of needs.

That's when Drogan changed.

He'd already been sneaking me sweet things, both literal and figurative. As soon as he knew though, he's been...

Good. He's been so good.

I wish he'd stop. I can't excise the fear spreading through me like a cancer; *I know how this ends.* By now, he has to know too.

The beep of his card against the scanner brings me to full focus. Drogan's face is nearly back to his usual mask of hot impassiveness when he guides me inside my humble abode, where I'm celled with real criminals. Unlike some of them, I did nothing to end up here. When I arrived here, I was *innocent.* My stomach sinks with the knowledge that that time is long gone.

Just before he straightens, Drogan's façade cracks, and he winks at me. His fingers brush against mine, and I meet his eyes. I appreciate the contact—this little connection.

I didn't expect this. He's all foul-mouth and rough edges at showing it, but Drogan *cares* about me.

He cares about me like I've been trying not to care about him.

This is bad. This is wrong.

He shouldn't try to make it easier for me. He should be furious. We both know they're going to make me kill him.

CHAPTER 2

PRETA

THE SUPER SOLDIER PROJECT could be what it's called. I've no idea what it's actually labelled; I'm not important enough to warrant showing me my own file. Although, with whatever they dope me down with during some experiments, they could wave my file in front of my face and I wouldn't be able to read it. Most times, I can't even stop myself from drooling. I can only lie there, and listen to their commentary as they run their little tests.

"Your family record is impressive. You must be a hell of a disappointment."

Contrary to cliché, our dad never wanted us to feel obligated to go into the military, or to become a decorated Green Beret or be inducted as a super spy. He tried to give us all the normalcy and assurances he could; he tried to make us secure in the knowledge that our choices were our choices. His efforts weren't in vain, because I never did feel obligated. My sister, Charlie, felt pulled. But not me. I had no interest, and zero aptitude.

"Your scores are deplorable. You're the perfect candidate: peak physical condition, aware of techniques, but technically unskilled. You're a diamond in the rough. Raw clay, just waiting to be formed."

The part about being aware of techniques is true. Our dad took us out and showed both Charlie and me all sorts of things. Before, I wasn't physically ideal as a candidate for anything. Not until they started the experiments on me. I knew something was wrong when I suddenly had the urge to jog for miles.

Me.

Jog.

The *urge* to *jog*.

Downright unnatural. That more than anything proved I'd lost *me*.

I'm glad my family will never see me like this.

They wouldn't recognize me.

I don't even recognize me.

The skin over my knuckles splits as it meets the woman's teeth. Ick. The bacteria in human mouths is disgusting. It *would* cause an infection considering I don't have easy access to first aid supplies—but I don't have to worry. Yet another perk to my forced chemical-injection upgrades: I heal well, and fast. I would know—the 'medical team' has made sure to inflict damage on me to test my recovery time.

I'm like their little pet guinea pig.

Most of us are, but as far as I can tell, we're all enrolled in different sideshows. I think I'm sort of the closest to the Strongman in this freak circus. I always thought the scene in that old cyborg movie, the second one, where the Sarah character racks the shotgun using only a one-handed grip, was SO cool. Our dad let us try that move, and you have to respect the dedication to pulling off a reload like that; it takes serious muscle. I couldn't do it then.

Now? After treatments, I *feel* like I could bend the barrel of a shotgun into a u-shape with my bare hands. In reality, that'd be a *no*—but I can lift some things that I wouldn't have been able to before, and the team seems very interested in this change. They're testing something with a social factor, that much I know; the *purpose* is the mystery.

I don't know the extent of this new drug yet, but after they dose me for the day, the side-effects—excess energy and hypersexuality—nearly have me climbing the walls in here.

I feel very alone. I have a desperate need to make connection, but also a desperate amount of dread, because every friend I make in here has been targeted.

It's like I can't stop myself though. I try, I *try* not to—I'm not mean, I just don't hang out the friendly-shingle either. But the good ones are drawn to me. It's always the good ones.

Zoya. Quinn. Lydia. Yahiro.

Yahiro hasn't been taken away—yet. She watches, but she's remained aloof; so collected, so cool under pressure, she reminds me of my sister. She is quieter than Charlie ever could be with me, but that isn't a bad thing in Alpha pod. I keep waiting for the guards to crack down on the talking, the socializing between inmates. I've heard from transfers that each sector of the ship is run a little differently, either worse or *worst,* from the sounds of it.

But the guards don't, and it's weird, so I have to believe it has a purpose.

Ever since Zoya and Quinn were dragged away it's gnawed at me—this is beyond loneliness. It sounds too farfetched but the research team *did* something to me, gave me an intense, *bizarre* desire to operate as something more than just... me. This must be what a hive insect feels like. This has to be why they keep tossing me back in the main cell here. Unfortunately, but perhaps by no coincidence, the new batch of chicas clad in orange are opposed to cozying up to me. It leaves me intensely frustrated, and even knowing it isn't natural, even though I have no constructive goal in mind, I'm stuck with this great desire to... 'people,' I guess.

I swipe at my nose with the back of my wrist. *Not bleeding, just feels like it.* It's a damn shame that my fellow inmates don't share my new-found interest in convivial behavior.

A retaliatory fist comes flying in my direction. I block, and I hit her again. The next time she swings, I catch her arm.

Dad had a 1973 Dodge Charger. In a world where vehicles were no longer constrained to four wheels and a strip of pavement, it was an oddity. And no, this was no replica kit car built on some other chassis; she was the real deal—and she had a real Charger-bitch temperament too. To get her to stay operational, he had to work on her all the time. This wasn't some museum floor piece: he had a temperamental, always-a-work-in-progress beauty that he went to the garage to bang on whenever he felt like cussing a blue streak.

Our dad is the epitome of the self-possessed male: level-headed, calm, cool—except for when it came to 'coaxing' that car. I was an impressionable seven-year-old who assumed that cunt and bitch were terms you applied to someone or something that you liked very much, but was frustrating you. My first grade teacher set me straight with a demerit and a visit to the principal's office, for which my father shook his head and tugged me to the spot between his knees, so that he could lean over me and whisper for my ears only, "You can't use those words. Even if I use them. You can't do everything I do yet, okay?"

I'd find out I'd never be able to do everything Dad did.

I thought breaking wrists was one of those things.

I was wrong.

Inmate 1525 screams so shrilly that she sounds like a macaque monkey. More than the feeling of her bones shattering under the pressure, *this* is what disturbs me. It's this noise she's making that snaps me out of my numbed-down state. My reaction to her attack started with an indignant flare-up of anger, but before I made the first move, it's like it got harnessed, and even now, I could be scrubbing burnt cheese off the bottom of an oven for all the excitement I feel in this moment.

Subduing her feels like a tired job.

I look around, taking note of the others watching us, seeing if any of her friends want to try shoving me to the floor. They're like jackals at the fringes, watching the hyenas and lions tear each other apart, and waiting to see if any of the entrails and scraps the victor leaves behind are worth picking over. Although I've gotten used to the scents in here, in this moment my senses are heightened to such an ultralight trigger pressure that I can even pick out the slightly burnt odor to the air—compliments of the laser bars that pass across the length of our cell. No steel bars for us: we get a force field. Like a wireless fence for a dog yard. And like dogs, I could gain pack status right now if I tried. But I don't want to be a lead dog. I just want to *belong* to something.

Ugh. That sounds pathetically needy.

I drop 1525's arm, and I don't even wince at how her hand now dangles useless and grotesque, like a broken puppet's. My thoughts are mostly mercenary: *she was a threat. Threat neutralized.*

The thud of booted feet breaks through the buzzing murmurs of the other inmates.

I sigh.

Electricity surges through me, and I'm frozen in place until the current abruptly cuts off.

I promptly crash face down. While I'm incapacitated, cuffs secure my wrists, and it's Drogan's *tsk* that I hear in my ear. It's his heat against my skin, his weight over me. I'd relax, but my body is still misfiring from the voltage.

Speaking of—*what is up* with this voltage?! The guard batons are basically cattle prods on steroids. This isn't the first, or the second, or even the fifth time I've been taken down by one, so I've had the time and opportunity to wonder; what's bigger than a cow? Bison. It's gotta be a bison prod. This can't be legal. Bison are huge, and they really do stampede—I get that it takes a massive wallop from an electric source to remind *bison* to respect the boundaries, but talk about cruel and unusual: I am nowhere close to the size of a bison—not even a weaned bison *calf.* These sticks must be set to 'fry'—they are *so* much stronger than they have to be.

"Preta," he breathes in a tone that reveals his regret. When he's on shift, he does what he can to stop these fights from escalating to this point. We both know this was unpleasant, but we also know him being the one to get to me first is a mercy—he doesn't abuse and prolong the punishment, not like some of these guards in here.

Case in point: his assigned partner on this shift is really, really eager to help. "I want in on some of this action." *Yuck.* Just the sound of this guy's voice makes my skin try to shrivel up and scamper off. "Here, give her to me. I'll take her to solitary."

He put an unnecessary and wholly unwanted emphasis on the last half of his suggestion. What a creeper. 'I'll *take her to* 'solitary,' hur-hur!'

"Naw, man—I got her."

Creeper-guard laughs and it is an *ugly* sound, and he's making me feel like the bad-dirty, not the hot-dirty, and I want a shower. Again, if my poor skin were capable of completely crawling off of my body, it would. At present, my skin and I are recovering from the brush with the electric fence-in-a-stick, so lying here placidly and unable to defend myself are about the extent of my abilities.

"Oh, you've *had* her." *(Hur-hur!)* "Let somebody else have a turn."

Great. More prison politics and drama. As much as I'm crazed for a release from the sexual tension that's been plaguing me with the latest round of drugs, I'm not all that excited at the prospect of being this guard's plaything. *No thanks.* Not ever. I'll masturbate in front of a room full of women who want to see me dead before I willingly go off alone with this guy.

Willing I am not, however; I *am* at the mercy of the guards, and Drogan is the only one here who cares what happens to me. I've heard some of the women—and other guards for that matter—they think I'm fucking Drogan in order to retain some form of protection. Which... from the standpoint of *survival,* isn't a half-bad idea, really. That wasn't my goal, or my intent, but right now, I am grateful he feels a sense of protectiveness towards me, and I don't care what motivates his chivalry: pussy, or pregnancy, or both. I'm just glad to have *someone* who has my back. It's been difficult not to have that security. I think maybe that's been one of the most difficult adjustments I've had to face; Charlie didn't just have my back—she always pushed me behind her and stood *in front* of me. To have that level of trust in another person's loyalties is priceless. I miss her presence with a keenness that makes it hard to breathe sometimes.

Although, I have experienced a small reprieve lately because I've started to feel more and more numb to it all. Temporary gifts from the laboratory?

Definitely not feeling numb now.

Fear hasn't settled in my gut yet, but it is working its way down the back of my neck, raising all the hairs there as Drogan attempts to avoid a scenario in which I get dragged off and molested if not outright raped.

More booted steps approach, and I feel the shift in my brain, like my super soldier senses are coming back online. Except this time, I don't know what they mean. I tense—a feat which proves I've regained the use of my own muscles.

"Guard 0072?"

That's Drogan's number.

He must nod, or show some sign of acknowledgement—or maybe he doesn't. From their hard, sadistic-flavored, *smug* tone, it's obvious they know exactly who he is, and what he's been to me.

"You're to come with us."

Drogan's warm fingers brush against my cuffed palms, which are flopped limply on my back, before he moves to stand over my prone body.

The air silently crackles. There'd be more luck sawing through a two-by-four with a butter knife than trying to cut the tension in this room right now, but even in this moment my libido proves it's completely out of control because this protective stance he's taking? *Hot.*

"Let me process—"

"Inmate SS-48 is being taken into custody also."

See? *SS:* Super Soldier, I'm telling you.

My injected skillset does me no good now though as I'm hauled up and frog marched alongside Drogan towards the exit. I sweep a calculating glance over the throng—and my outwardly calm appearance is not a pretense. Right now, I feel like I've gone dead inside. *This is it.* Drogan got protective over me one too many times—*despite* being the one to nail me with the bison stick more than once, I might add—there were too many little instances where he showed me favoritism.

He's going to die for it.

Unlike my friends who were dragged in the direction of the labs, never to be seen again, guards get a special treatment.

Drogan knows it too: his shoulders are back and his chin is up and his silent sigh is resigned. All eyes are on us, and it's eerie how their whispers blend together to make a background-noise hiss, the undercurrent of excitement unmistakable; we certainly are putting on a show for the ladies here in cell block whatever-this-sector is.

"It was nice knowing you," he murmurs to me as they herd us out and into the corridor.

"Likewise." I swallow, and now I do feel a tiny sliver of pain to the region of my heart before it's abruptly cut off—it's almost as if my system attacks it and replaces it with a sense of calm. "I'm sorry."

Out of the corner of my eye, I see his grim smile. "Same here. If we'd known I was going to die today anyway, we could have enjoyed that second fuck."

CHAPTER 3

PRETA

THIS PRISON SHIP HAS been cruising above Earth for something like ten years. It made big news back when it was launched. It didn't matter to me much then. It didn't affect my life at all, actually—not until I became a pawn.

Charlie is a soldier. Our dad's a soldier. Both of them really *are* super soldiers—but not the laboratory-engineered kind. They're entirely where they are today through God-given-talent and hard work. Both have access to all sorts of sensitive knowledge in plots that make the whole world run smoother, blah, blah—there are big things that they no doubt have big parts in orchestrating: blah. They're the behind-the-scenes-heroes you only hear about in movies.

There's no 'blah' to that part. That part's just cool.

I think Charlie's mom was really a spy. That's my best theory. Honestly, I wouldn't rule it out for Grandma Sol either; two dominant, awesome-spy genes converging in our dad, thereby doubling up the action for Charlie's nucleus down the line would make a lot of sense.

My mom must have basically been a true normal, because I was quite average in a long line of greats—but I was happy with that. Happy to be an unwitting civilian who loved two people who did secret things to make the world a little safer. I didn't know what those things were, and as long as *they* were safe, I didn't care, and didn't care to know their various mission deets. Their secret lives didn't affect me; their job details didn't matter. Not to me.

Someone made it matter. Someone is playing a game and I don't get to see the whole board, or the stakes, or the other players—I don't even know what this game is called, because again—I'm just a pawn.

Someone is trying to hurt our dad, or Charlie, or both. I'm here because I'm leverage, and whoever's running the show thinks they can control two *legit* super soldiers (the trained, real battle-tested kind, not the made-by-injection kind) by threatening their soft spot. The whys of it aren't important anymore; this has gone beyond a simple threat—I'm *on* this prison ship, and I've been here for six months. The fact that I'm still incarcerated here means that hell has frozen over. My family is not one to screw with, and their loyalty is vast and unshakable. Whoever pulled strings to get and keep me here is going to have a world of hurt rain down on them, and I'm sure my family is probably burning down cities in their efforts to get me out—I *know* they are—but in the meantime, things aren't so good here.

Drogan's been adjusting his stride for the purpose of keeping pace with me as we're forced towards the laboratory. Dimly, I register that it's dread that's pooling in my stomach. This isn't the first guard who's been recorded as 'dying in a prison riot,' or whatever they put on the paperwork at the end of the day.

But he is the only guard who I've trusted enough to initiate sex with.

He's also the only man I've made a tiny person with.

We never really spoke of it, because although we tried to hide so we wouldn't get caught fucking, we still feared audible monitoring to an extent.

At least, that's why I never brought it up.

Well... that's *one* of the reasons I never brought it up. I've also been, from the moment I realized I was pregnant, fully aware that I wouldn't be allowed to keep this baby. I thought, with the crap they pump into me, that it was unlikely I'd get to carry this little life to term, let alone deliver.

I would have been terrified for my child—*our* child—but I assumed they'd terminate it as soon as they found out, and if they terminate its life before it's born, at least it means they won't be testing on it. No matter what happens, I know I can't do a thing to protect it unless I go free.

And if that hasn't already happened...

I'm pretty sure they don't wrongly imprison an innocent woman, test on her, alter her, and then turn her loose to tell-all to the media.

My future's looking kinda bleak.

When I'm no longer useful to them, I expect to wind up very dead.

Because with my family's skills, let alone resources, whoever's behind this would be damn fools to do what they've done to me and then send me back home with an apology note clipped to my collar. No, they might be trying to use me to force my family into doing whatever they want done, but they have no intention of letting me go afterwards. In the meantime, they're making the best use of me that they can.

Unless my theory is correct. My blood crystallizes in my veins as I consider the strength with which I believe that they've known all along about my pregnancy: bone deep. The team all seemed very enthusiastic about their job—they freaking love their job—and they've haven't gotten to dig into me in weeks. It's *not* a coincidence.

Only a reprieve.

I shudder.

Drogan's shoulder brushes against mine.

Also not a coincidence.

I meet his eyes, and I'm nearly suffocated with a serious wave of frustration. I *like* Drogan. It's painful—like blood flow reawakening tissues nearly destroyed by frostbite.

Whatever they've done to me, they put in a switch: when I have to defend myself, or when I have to follow an order, I don't suffer, wondering if what I had to do was good or bad. It was *necessary*. Whatever moral agony I would have felt in my old life has been stripped.

Facing Drogan, something is changing—chemical suppression override, or something. Probably due to pregnancy hormones rocking the boat.

I wonder if they factored *that* into their little experiment.

We're ushered into a high-tech exam room, decorated in delightfully drab gray but even worse than plain, drab grays are the bright and colorful features: high powered lights, locked cabinets of drugs with noxious yellow warning labels, and shelves of equipment, beakers, vials, and *instruments*.

I hate the instruments.

Drogan gets restrained. I get those sticky nodes affixed to my forehead, under my shirt, and at my wrist. No doubt the team noted every reaction and heartbeat as they made me murder strangers. Now, they'll get to monitor my every reaction and heartbeat while they make me murder someone I *like*.

Extra distressing is that I *feel distress*—if ever there is a time for their forced numbing, I need it now—because without a shadow of a doubt, I know I'll be literally powerless to stop what happens next. Once they give me the order, I'll kill. I don't know what they did to me to install it, but I'm remote-control activated: if I hear a specific phrase, it flips a switch in my brain and I destroy my target.

It begins with a calmly uttered, "See the antlers on that stag?" So innocuous, my command to murder. Simple. And I'm helpless to do anything but follow it. They know this well. What they don't expect is for me to possess any control of *who* I carry out the kill order on.

I've never given them any reason to think I have some control. I don't have enough to do me any good, but I must have inherited a latent copy of the secret agent gene, because very early on here, it expressed itself by internally cautioning me to bide my time just in case I ever needed to flex my tiny loophole: I do not in fact, have to *immediately* kill who they sic me on.

This doesn't sound like a lot of wiggle room—it isn't. But it's *something,* and if I'd revealed this early on, they would have tightened their control, cut off my tiny ability to rebel, and I'd have nothing now.

That said, I can't fool myself; Drogan isn't walking out of here, and neither am I. I haven't been saving up for a grand escape: we're in a prison ship in the sky. *There is* no escape.

This right here is a suicide mission at best, and a total loss of self and self-control once they figure out how to stop-gap me. If we live through this, they're just going to repeat this entire exercise in order to test that they've perfected it. Drogan will face me as his firing squad again, and this will all be for nothing.

They'll tie up the next poor sucker who swiped late for his shift one too many times, or they'll bring me a prisoner who they've run out of uses for, and they'll make me kill them too.

To think that I was innocent of any crime when I arrived here, and now, with the things I've been programmed to do, I actually deserve to be locked away. After this, they'll break me of any spare inch of free will I have left. I need to make this good. We've got one shot, but we've also got a guaranteed bad ending.

My body is vibrating with the need to lunge at the 'stag.' My breath catches with the sinking realization that I don't have as much control as I believed I did. *I can't turn* from Drogan—I can only resist.

This all changes when one of guards off to the side of me shifts slightly, eyeing me. That small movement is our saving grace; my focus breaks from Drogan, and I launch myself on the guard instead.

Blink. I have his gun. *Blink.* One bullet between the eyes—he's dropped. *Repeat, repeat, rep—*

When it's Drogan's raised hands that I see in the sights, I swing past him and onto the next target—a tech that was incredibly fond of the stainless steel torture makers a.k.a the contents of the instrument tray. I can't say the same. *Blink.* He's down—far quicker than he deserves.

The acrid smell of firing propellant is irritating my senses so completely that it causes me to pause in my killing spree. My focus slips from my mission, to my surroundings, and I'm startled to hear Drogan.

"Do *not* shoot me," his tone is authoritative. "The clearing is *empty*."

A new command. The bastard knows how to unlock sequences in my brain that I didn't even know existed—and in the time it takes me to marvel at this, I've crossed the floor and am wielding one of these handy scalpels in order to cut through the zip ties that were used to secure him.

"*Neutralized*," he breathes, and I relax.

Weird.

He's referring to the threats in the room. I look around with him.

Everyone but us is dead.

The floor beneath us jars so violently that I pitch forward and narrowly miss crashing through a stand of beakers and Bunsen burners. I stick to the wall: not because I'm trying to stay upright and out of the way, but because it's like I've been sucked into the old amusement park ride *The Gravitron*—I *can't* peel myself from the wall of cabinets and racks. A buzzing sound fills my ears as the lights flicker—

WHOOoooSH!

There is a roar so loud, it temporarily drowns out the screams that carry through the door.

What's happening?

Long, long ago, there was this ship full of people. This ship went down in infamy forever when it crashed into an iceberg, and sentenced most of its passengers to a horrifying, watery grave.

I don't need to be one of the geniuses on the floor to know that a hit like we just took—or whatever's just happened—isn't good.

Sure, we're not in a ship that floats in the water—we're flying through the air.

Or we *were*.

CHAPTER 4

PRETA
SOMETHING IS VERY WRONG.

Drogan and I are armed to the teeth—every weapon we could strap on is taking a ride on us as we exit the lab. I almost changed into one of the guard's uniforms simply for the purpose of having easy access to holsters and loaded pockets, but with the noises and alarms outside this room, I feel too rushed to take the time.

"I take point," Drogan informs me.

Identified lead soldier, fall into formation!

...That's not evil-scientist programming. That's conditioning from a military first-person shooter game I used to play with Charlie.

I laugh a little to myself as I shake my head to regain focus. Drogan is looking at me curiously now, but I'm not going to argue—especially when I see his eyes drop to my stomach. If the man wants to act as our shield... I'm going to let him act as our shield.

I'm disgusted at how content I feel as I fall into step behind him.

We're a team.

Cold fingers of dread dig into the edges of my nerves as he swipes his badge, and can't get the door to activate.

"They wasted no time in sweeping you out of the system," I murmur.

He curses. "I need one of the other guard's passes." He gives my appearance a double take. "Your hair's all fucked up, Sol."

Unlike Charlie's, my hair behaves pretty well. (On a *normal* day—spaceship shake-ups notwithstanding.) She must get the crazy-curlage from her mom. Despite mine being easier to maintain, without

27

access to a mirror, mine feels like it's all over the place. "No shampoo commercial scouts are going to sign me on," I say in defeat, but Drogan reaches over and finger-combs it into place for me, and the smile he slants me makes me feel a little better. Still filthy, but better.

A dead guard gets badge-stripped: it works! I nudge Drogan out of the way to tap some fun things into the card reader.

"Do you know what the fuck you're doing?"

I shoot him a warning look. "You did not just take that tone with me. I'm saving our ass. Shut up so I can hear the instructions my brain weirdly knows."

His mouth quirks up, but he doesn't open it again.

He does put his hand on my lower back though. It's an oddly... affectionate gesture.

"Completed," I declare, and with a nod, he takes the lead he so gallantly called.

We step out of the room only to enter into *madness.* Pure madness.

A very-much-alive guard, bristling with aggression to disguise half the panic that's causing his upper lip and forehead to profusely sweat, points to us and thunders, "Secure your fuck-toy, Drogan!"

Fuck-toy? Who all knows about Drogan and me? If *everybody* knew we were having sex, we could have had that round two, or maybe even three—

Drogan doesn't miss a beat. He turns smoothly, still blocking the guard's view of me, giving me time to relocate the gun in my hands into one of my pockets. Jumpsuits are ugly, but I'm giving mine a giant (silent) huzzah for being useful for once. If these were a pair of pants, I'd be worried about them sliding off of me. Guns are heavy.

So are cuffs, which Drogan 'secures' me with promptly afterward.

"Ship crashed," the guard at his back spits.

Drogan and I go still.

"Get her back to her block. The generators are keeping the cell's weave active, but we've already had to shoot a couple to calm down a riot. But we have plans to fix their shit."

That doesn't sound good.

A muscle in Drogan's jaw ticks, and his eyes catch mine.

I can't give him anything. I can't reassure him, and he can't avoid putting me back in.

His eyes are saying it all: *we're so fucked.*

THE GUARDS' COLLECTIVE, brilliant plan is to send a few unlucky persons—a.k.a. cannon fodder—out into the alien landscape where we've crashed. That's right. *Alien* landscape. Science has never been my thing, but *'wormhole,'* is the whispered explanation I'm catching from the chatter going on around me. One minute, we were orbiting Earth, and the next...

The crash tore the Alpha pod completely off the *Concord;* who knows where the rest of it ended up? We don't know if there are survivors. We don't know how far away the remains of the other pods on the ship might be, nor do we know the state of the *supplies* in those pods.

We desperately need the supplies.

The food and water were contaminated, or blew up—nobody cares about filling in the details for us prisoners. A few of the guards have taken it upon themselves to emerge as leaders, and they're marching us, and barking, and the gist of their noise is: don't panic and *shut up.*

It's dark, and creepy, but thanks to the ship, we've got some floodlights, which manage to provide exactly enough illumination into the forest to scare the bejeesus out of us.

A tree off to my right is dripping a slightly opaque substance off of its branches like a Saint Bernard slobbers. A naked, wrinkled green beastie with scary hook-like hands clings to the underside of a branch, gobbling up everything its little mouth can catch, and its stomach is expanding right before our very eyes. It looks like it could almost pop—

It explodes.

We all throw ourselves down to the ground, with various exclamations of horror.

This is *not* Earth.

"Get your asses up!" comes the thoroughly unfriendly request. "If you want to live, you'd best start walking when we tell you to walk and find out what won't kill you."

That's right: we're test dummies. The researchers who cared about the welfare of their various pet projects aren't out here fighting for our safety. In fact, they're conspicuously nowhere to be seen. I know mine are all a little dead, and maybe the others' are too—either that, or they moved from Alpha pod before we crashed. I don't know where the rest of the ship is, but we are definitely on our own with the guards, who seem to have a very different take on our usefulness. *They* aren't going to risk dying from a poisonous berry, or eating explosive tree slime. Total cowards.

I stare at what looks like one of the beastie's hook-hands as it twitches in the burned grass a few feet from us.

All right... I can't blame them for that last one—I'm staying the hell away from that tree too.

"There is NO way I'm going in that forest!" an inmate shrieks.

I don't normally agree with the prisoners, but right now, I'm *so* with her on this. I am *not* going any deeper into this place.

She's still screaming. "You can't make—"

The bullet kills her before the discharge from the handgun even registers as a sound.

I've always wanted to see the jungle.

These guys could teach classes on settling disputes; I don't speak only for myself when I say that watching this has instantly instilled an invigorating air of motivation.

"Look at that," the guard drawls. "When the others get their bitches here, we'll have five in each group. Doesn't that work slick?"

Does he expect us to clap?

"You, the bony whore: get over here."

Everyone looks at me.

Well.

When I don't immediately move, he uses the gun to both direct me and remind me that my choices are *follow* or *die*. Stiffly, I force myself to approach him. This is how Drogan finds me: being given the choice between eating the berries the guard has shoved at me, or eating a bullet.

The berries are a little bitter.

"What the fuck, man!" Drogan is shouting at this boss-guard. "She's on a special regimen! She gets the Project-45s. What the hell are you making her eat?"

The boss-guard dismisses this with simple but factual logic: "This one's got nothing left to her." He follows this with a disturbing, distressing, somewhat erroneous plan: "If shit's poisonous, she'll be the first to get it through her system and drop, right? We can use her to test out what food is safe to eat *tonight*."

My job here is to eat food and live, or eat food and die, and until it hits my stomach and causes one of those two outcomes to either continue or *end* my reality, my work for the moment is on hold, thus the boss-guard doesn't protest when Drogan drags me away. Drogan is a man though, and he's doing that man-thing where he glares down his opponent—even as we're retreating—and if he doesn't quit, he's going to get himself killed.

I hate to do it, but I try to break his side of the staredown. "He was so thoughtful. He even took my cuffs off first, see?" He doesn't look, but that's okay, I keep talking. "He didn't even make me forage for the creepy berries—they were growing right next to where the ship crashed, totally unharmed! I'm *so* lucky."

"It's not fucking funny!" Drogan snaps, but his eyes flicker down to me, worried, and it's just enough of a concession that the boss-guard can walk away with his ego and pride fully intact.

I'm sorry, Drogan.

Drogan's glare locks on the man's back.

"Let it go," I whisper.

I go unheard. Or at least unheeded.

"Permission to retrieve the inmates' Project Rations," he calls out. To me, he mutters under his breath, "Killing *all* the doctors may have been a bad call."

"We didn't kill all the doctors. We didn't kill all of the scientists either," I quickly add, figuring what he'll try to come back with. I experience a rapid series of flashbacks. Slowly, I shake my head. "And *no*. It was *not*."

He drags an impatient hand over his hair, but his voice sounds a *little* amused by my antics. As he should. They're on his behalf, after all. "All of *your* docs and scientists then—fucking hell woman, you fight with me like we're friggin' married."

"You should be so lucky," I tease.

When he looks down at me... he... is not teasing anymore. "I should be."

Wait... *"What?"*

Drogan's smile disappears, and his eyes flick over me in an extremely concerned way, not a *'you're going to make me fuck you against this ship if you don't shut up'* way.

I was all for this option. Just for the record.

It's like I can *see* his stress redouble. I'm guessing it's become even more noticeable, the effect of my 'enhanced metabolism.' It's been accelerated; like he said, the team had to put me on a special diet and schedule and everything—without their tender loving care and monitoring, I'm already starting to feel like a hummingbird that hasn't been able to find any flowers. If I don't get what my body needs and soon, I could waste away from hunger, and it will happen much quicker than to a normal human. The baby situation probably isn't doing my body any favors in that department either. I look down at myself, and even I can tell I'm already looking rough.

Boss-guard pivots slowly and says, "Lab's locked. Damnedest thing. Nobody can get in. Bet you wouldn't know anything about that."

Wisely, Drogan says nothing.

"We'll get it open. Don't know when that'll be, but tell you what. If we *can't* get to it in time, maybe we'll give you the chance to get one last ride out of her." With that, the ass saunters away.

I tackle Drogan before he can attack the man from behind. "Get it together!" I hiss into his ear.

He roars like an *animal.*

At me!

He lets me spin him around, and glares down at me while I challenge him. I catch his sleeve, the clingy-affectionate-*supplicating* move at odds with my sarcastic tone. "I'm sorry, *sir.*"

Oh, he likes this.

Enjoying the heat in his eyes now, I put my hands on his chest. "I don't speak in *tiger.* What was that order you just snarled at me?"

He releases one of those man-growl breaths and it would sound super sexy if it weren't me that he was aiming it at. I eye the width of his broad shoulders, taking in his pissed-but-still-hot look.

Hm. Maybe sexy aimed at me after all.

"You're starving. *You two are starving to death* right before my eyes." *You two.*

I check my hand before I can touch my stomach.

"And don't eat anything else," he warns me.

I give him the look that this asinine order deserves. "And when they move to shoot me, you'll take the bullet?"

"YES."

"And when you're dead?"

I get another man-growl for my trouble, but I also get a bicep squeeze that hopefully looks like he's doing his duty and bossing me around, because it sure *feels* reassuring and very... fond.

I can tell from the killing glares I'm getting from my fellow inmates that whatever it looks like, they think I've got it better than them.

I'm so going to get shivved.

I give Drogan a moment before I pull away, and walk ahead of him. When I return to the rest of the inmates, I am yet again disgusted with the part of my brain that is happy for an honest-to-God group-based activity, even if we are facing certain death stranded on a strange planet with creepy creatures and trigger happy guards.

Maybe it's the cold turkey off the project treatment cocktail that my body has gotten used to being provided with by now, but I feel very strange. I space out, just for a second, an image of Charlie popping up front and center in my mind. I can almost hear her voice. Being distracted could get me eaten by a facehugger or something; I need to stay sharp, but I can't force myself to stop from spinning around anyway, even as I'm thinking, *this is exactly how I'm going to get grabbed, it'll be by some deadly creature while I'm busy looking for—*

"CHARLIE!" I shriek.

Two things: I'm not crazy, because Charlie really *is* right here, she is not a figment of my overactive or overstressed imagination, and when she throws her arms around me, her cuffed hands hooking the back of my neck, I smugly think, *I wasn't* wrong—*this IS a deadly creature.*

After all, this is my badass sister.

Grinning, squeezing her hard, I'm jarred by the sudden realization that I'm *feeling.* Warmth, relief, worry, affection, and sadness—this last one because if Charlie is here, in *prison,* she wrecked her life—her *career*—heck, with what they'd have to do in order to crack a person as strong as Charlie?—her *sanity* in order to save me.

And oh how entertaining she'd have been. A shiny, tough, brave, fascinating toy. Of course they'd want to play with her.

Aw, Charlie.

When she pulls back, I know exactly what she's seeing, and I know she's going to worry, so I'm compelled to jump in with sisterly love. I peer at her raccoon mask. "How's your side of the accommodations in Alpha pod? My room service doesn't fold the towels into swans and I'm going to write to the head of the company about it."

She goes in for another hug, and I know shit's serious. Sure, my underfed appearance isn't helping, but another lesson our dad taught us? Everybody can be broken. Charlie is *so strong.*

Right now, she doesn't look it.

It's *killing* me.

I aim to tease her out of this mood. I start by eyeing her suit. "You look like a fucking radioactive pumpkin."

The sadness and pain in her eyes flickers for a brief beat as her lips twitch. "I think what you mean is I look like I'm *fucking* a radioactive pumpkin."

I let my brows climb. "It does look like the orange thing is *on* you. And with your hair—*damn,* girl. I'd say you look good in blaze orange, but I've heard there are good things in the afterlife. I don't want to be barred from the fun for telling an untruth of these proportions."

She glances down at herself. "For your information, I believe this shade is more politely referred to as *'saffron.'*"

"Like... *'sorry I'm affronted* by that eyesore-shade?' *'Saffronted,* saffron. I can see it," I say, smiling even as I mock contemplate—because Charlie's whooping with laughter now, and it's good to hear, and for now, for just this moment, it's normal again. Everything's okay. She's not hurting, and I'm not... not what I've turned into, and she didn't just fuck up her life to rescue me, and we're not both stranded on an alien planet.

"Preta," she gasps, still bent at the waist, her hands on her knees from where she was slapping them a moment before, enjoying the briefest spark of hilarity.

"Don't," I whisper. My throat is already tight.

She nods and straightens. "Yeah."

Not ready to return to the grimness of our situation yet, I eye her. "Since when do you know fancy names for fashion colors?" I can tell I drive her nuts, and I love it. I miss it. I don't like how haunted she looks. "And what'd they do to you during your stay at *casa de* torture chamber? Fun things?"

"It was the vacation I'd never dreamed of."

A hand lands on her shoulder and yanks her backwards, and just like that, reality gives us the bum-rush.

It provides a learning opportunity though; Charlie's expression doesn't flicker as she nails her guard in the face using her elbow, and I can *hear* his nose break. This is why my sister is my hero—she's just *cool*.

"Impressive!" I call to her, but she's in the zone and I don't think she hears me.

Apparently, I should have stopped gawking and paid more attention to our surroundings—*'Points off for lack of situational awareness,'* as our dad would tease—because I don't see the two guards until they're nearly on top of Charlie. She's up on the balls of her feet, her muscles coiling, shoulders squaring as she prepares to take them head-on. I see more of them spilling from the ship—baton sticks out. My heart flatlines. Bullets might be permanent but I've seen enough prisoners die to know that at least most of the time it's as close to instantaneous as any death gets. Voltage though? You can't fight against it, and unfortunately, these guys are pros: they'll make us *wish* we were dead.

I hate these sticks.

If Charlie had a distraction, she could take them and we—

A guard pulls out his pistol.

Okay, I hate the sticks, they make us wish for death, etcetera, etcetera, so on and so forth but no matter how much I complain, bullets *are* worse. It's the whole permanency thing. I don't want my sister dead!

This time, I only whisper, but *this* time, she does hear me: "Charlie, *don't*."

She looks torn, confused even, and in that moment the men perform a tackle worthy of taking down a four hundred pound quarterback.

Assholes!

"Don't hurt her!"

They rub her face in the dirt like a bad dog on carpet.

I slam my fist into the throat of the guard that's *kneeling* on my sister's *back*.

"That'll be enough!" a guard almost jerks me off my feet.

I wish it had been Drogan that had found us. He'd have been able to break this up and mitigate the damage. The guy who holds me is riling up the guard with the broken nose, and the way that guy's glaring at Charlie says he has a grudge and a major score to settle. *Not good.* I sit down meekly, hoping they won't hurt her any worse, and then I see her smirk.

I breathe the biggest sigh of relief. Charlie may have taken a beating here.

But she's not broken.

SIGHING AND GRUMBLING, I spit on my knuckles, and wipe them on my suit. It's supposed to be self-cleaning. The government commissioned the design, trying to save money considering the water filtration needs of a spaceship of this size would be horrendous, but incidental bonus? This has probably saved most of us from a traumatizing Shawshank scene: no washdays, yay! But it's self-cleaning, not magic. Maybe in a few days the nanofibers or whatever makes it so it never has to be washed will be able to combat the worst of it, but until then? I'm covered in blood and dirt and honestly, all I want is a decent meal, a clean change of clothes, and a hot shower—and not in that order.

"What the hell happened to your hand?"

Tipping my head back and seeing Drogan's stormy expression makes me smile. "The way you just asked me that? I know that it was really manspeak for, 'Aww, baby, you're hurt, and it makes me concerned.'"

He huffs, and I *think* it's a laugh.

He surprises me when his voice pitches lower, and it still comes out rough, but it's tender when he tries again. "Awww, baby. Your hand is fucking hurt. I'm pissed. What happened?"

I don't huff. I *do* laugh. "I want to hug you right now, you dork."

He tugs me until we're standing off in the dark, just slightly apart from the group, and growls into my ear, "I want to do more than hug you."

YES. I want this too.

I want this very much.

One of the guards begins addressing everybody.

My vagina is silently crying *'DAMN IT!'*

I shift my weight, preparing to rejoin the suicide squad. "It looks like he's pontificating on important things we should know before they send the prisoners to forage."

Drogan catches my wrist and kisses my owwie. Germs and all. My heart kind of goes melty.

"Before you trot back there, how hot you feelin'? Scale one to ten."

He's not talking about a Miss America scale of hotness. He's talking about my out of control libido. He doesn't wait for my answer—he simply tows me along, and when I see that Charlie's got her eyes locked on the ground and that we're not going to be allowed to chat, I follow Drogan as he picks his way back to the ship, keeping just outside of the floodlights.

"My sister is here," I blurt, but I feel my excitement... dulling. Like the barred doors that roll down at night to protect shops in the mall. Charlie came to save me but I can't see a way for us to get home. She gave up everything to *try*, but we're both stuck. We don't even know what planet we crashed on, or where Earth is from here, which'll be kind of an important thing if the Alpha pod can be repaired enough for the rigors of takeoff and space travel.

Unlikely.

Drogan's pace stutters, but he doesn't break from guiding me along. "Your sister? *Both* of you are here? What the...?"

I force him to stop within the lit area so that I can see his face when I say, "What do you think I did to get here?"

Drogan has nice eyes. They look incredibly sad now as he gazes down at me. "Nothing that earned you this."

I feel my lips tip up. "You sound so sure."

The longer he stares at me, the less sad he appears, and the hotter his eyes get. "Get moving before we give everyone a show."

"*Oooh.* Yes, sir!"

He gooses me and when I slap a hand over my mouth in shock, he tosses me a smirk. "Oh yeah, hardened criminal."

He urges me forward and instead of taking us up one of the well-lit ramps, he sneaks us through the dark cargo doorway. I do trust him enough that I don't ask questions—at least, not until he seals the big door behind us, plunging us into complete blackness. "What are you—"

"Shhh. Relax," he breathes into my ear as he nuzzles my hair with his nose. "Or this is never going to work. And call me Ryan."

This shuts me up. *Ryan? Ryan Drogan.* I didn't know his first name. I didn't know the father of my baby's *name.*

"What's your middle name?" I ask, suddenly fighting a sense that we're running out of time.

He laughs softly into my suit as he lowers himself in front of me. "Later. For now, shut up, and let me take care of you."

As I spread my fingers over hair that is regularly acquainted with electric clippers, I take advantage of a sense of relaxation that I haven't enjoyed since pre-*Concord* as he delivers on his promise and provides me with assistance in reaching that orgasm that I've desperately needed.

"How do you feel?" he asks quietly.

"Like I don't need to kill anyone," I slur, and he rasps a chuckle.

"I meant with you being... how's our Drogan-Sol?"

I jolt. "Cute!" I shake my head and try to make him out in the darkness. "Fine. I'm fine. As far as I know, *we're* fine."

My skin jumps when my stomach is bared, his big rough hand sliding up to block my undershirt before I feel his lips pressing softly against my abdomen, and for the first time, it isn't sexual. How... odd.

Blink.

"Preta..."

I try to figure out what just happened. We're at the door—*I* brought us here. My hand is tightly wrapped as far around Ryan's thick wrist as my fingers can span, and I realize I *dragged* him here.

"What are those instincts urging you to do right now?" he asks, and I can hear unmasked curiosity.

"What do you know?" I counter.

There isn't even a pause. "I'm a grunt. They don't pay me to think, and they didn't care what I overheard. I think I know a lot. And I think your maternal instincts are coming online, manifesting and tweaking with that military strategy playbook in your head."

"Sounds about right," I start slowly. "My sister, Charlie... I want to grab her, and you, and... I want to be safe. I need all of us to be safe."

"And you're feeling threatened. And when I kissed your skin, near the baby, what happened?"

I feel my cheeks heat, and I'm glad he can't see. I try to break down what occurred between the moment his lips tenderly skated over my skin, and he's right—it's the baby. It stopped being sexual, and all I wanted to do was protect little *Drogan-Sol*... and Drogan-Sol's daddy. And aunt.

Drogan is following along without me voicing a thing, and his next words give me pause; he seems to have quite a grasp on motivations—*my* motivations—that even I don't fully understand. "It initiated like a protect-mode, and you want to move your unit away from the threat."

"Tell me something you know," I urge. "One thing."

Calloused fingers cup my chin. "I'll tell you everything I know," he promises.

"Now?"

His breath smells like me when he exhales a soft laugh against my face. "Your survival instinct is supposed to be higher than normal—you are supposed to absorb loss better, without the trauma. But yet, in theory, you'll retain your loyalty to your surviving unit. That said, the thought of self-sacrifice doesn't bother you, does it?"

The thought of it does not. "No."

He's hugging me now, and I can feel his chin booping the top of my head softly with his nod. "Right."

A little self-examination, and I can sense what he's talking about. I'd push Charlie down to take a bullet meant for her—but if it was a random inmate? Not 'part of my unit?'

I'd let her eat it, and I'd live another day.

It feels like it *should* feel cold, but I don't feel anything for the inmates—not the ones left here—there's no loyalty, no love lost, so there's none given.

"Someone with that trait would have an easier time during real war," Drogan offers. "And part of your research was to provide programming for soldiers so they could make the transition from active duty to civilian easier to cope with. Obviously, the research team will never see this side, but someday you'll be out of this, and safe, and your extra instincts will tone down. For now though, this is good."

"...Why is it good?"

"The odds of us getting out of this alive—"

"Don't say it."

"Preta, let's be real. If it comes down to me or you two?"

He's not talking Charlie.

"Pick you two, no matter if your instincts try to tell you otherwise."

My nails dig into his back, and Drogan's arms tighten around me, but I don't make him any promises.

I don't have to. He whispers into my ear, "Your head is telling you to be Team Baby Drogan-Sol, isn't it?"

I nod into his shoulder, and he hugs me tighter.

CHAPTER 5

PRETA

THE ONLY GOOD NEWS about the darkness is that even when we catch up to my group, it hides Drogan's proximity to me. His voice is low and hushed when he asks, "You know what would have been helpful?"

I squint off into the distance as if I can actually see through the black. "Being able to determine if questions were rhetorical?"

I get an amicable shoulder-slam before he continues over me. "Popping the plans into your head for things like ship repair."

"Wow, that would have been great. Thanks. Now I wish they'd have given me that instead of a set of phrases that turn me into a psycho killer bomb, ready to detonate on the unsuspecting."

I slap at whatever just stung my neck. It squishes between my fingers, and I add it to the collection of nasty that covers my jumpsuit. This is a *hostile* planet. And it's only getting more hostile the farther we're forced to walk into it. "That roar sounded way close," I groan—but *quietly*—I don't want to die—and Drogan's moved to my side, so he hears me just fine.

"You're not really a psycho," he defends absently.

Gee, he's too kind. I purse my lips at him, and I think he doesn't see until he squeezes my fingers.

"The head asshole doesn't want to pack this expedition up just yet." He sounds majorly pissed off about this. Probably because we can barely see the lights from the ship now, the noises of the wildlife are getting louder, not to mention closer, yet we haven't found a damn thing for food or water because it's *dark*.

43

All in all, this is a bust. "Because he thinks whatever beast can make sounds like that," I stab a finger in the direction of the scary creature-noise, "won't be able to find us without a flashlight? Speaking of: despite us having them, we're literally stumbling around out here. It's pretty much impossible to forage at night. What exactly does this head asshole expect us to do?"

"I don't fucking *know!*" he explodes in a furious whisper.

"Drogan gets growly when he gets scared," I muse. "And remember when I said that being able to determine when a question was rhetorical would be a helpful skill? I wasn't just talking about me."

A hand lands on my ribs and punishes me with the five-fingered spider-dance even as he claps a palm over my mouth so my protests are smothered.

An unholy scream rips through the air.

All around us, the flashlights that had been trained on the path ahead turn into panicked strobe light beams as the others try to pinpoint the what and the where of this sound's origin.

Drogan's hand clamps down over mine, keeping our lights static, keeping us still.

Unnecessary. I wasn't moving. I can't. My body has locked up as my programming informs me that moving targets attract attention.

But ha, take that, programming: I was trained by the best. I already knew this. This leads me to a thought though; what if my program is based off of missions my dad and sister were successful in? Like during debriefing, the things they shared that helped them succeed in missions have now been programmed into *me?* Just the possibility that it could, in some way, be connected to them makes me resent its presence in my head a little less.

At the very edge of our light, a woman stumbles—

SNAP!

And then it's just a shoe.

I think I saw teeth close over her. Lots and lots of teeth. It was so fast. The muffled sound of her screams devolves into a gurgle as something crunches down on her body.

Panic erupts. Everybody's running.

"Preta, *move!* I hid packs!" Drogan shouts. "Get back to the ship! We'll grab those!"

I'm all for his plan, but I'm more at a loss of how to execute it as we race along, inmates resembling orange wildebeest, all of us stampeding for the safety of the ship's lights.

The monsters aren't afraid of the lights though, and they're waiting for us here like we're the platters that are finally being served to their table.

"About those packs," Drogan says before he forces a string of curses through gritted teeth. "Forget 'em. C'mon!"

I move to follow him.

"Preta!"

The warning shout comes from behind us, and I know this voice.

I whirl around, and illuminate a *nightmare.*

If you took a Utahraptor, a rock python, and the creepiest freaking bug you could imagine, *this* is what it looks like.

But bigger.

It had been heading straight for me.

But now?

It's headed for Charlie.

No!

The look in her eyes—it's apology, and regret, and worry. She gives me one nod.

"PRETA! Your six 'o clock! We need to *go.*"

She can't make it to me, and our flashlights are not exactly a match against the things converging on us, so I find my head bobbing back, before my body mechanically turns, and I fall in with Drogan, both of us racing deeper into the woods.

CHAPTER 6

PRETA

DROGAN BREATHES, "TRY to hold still for a few seconds, then move slowly. Very slowly. Ghillie-suit slow."

Ghillie-suit: when soldiers wear their environment as camouflage and tactically engage at a creeping pace, blending so well, you never know they're there.

I'm in a blaze orange fucking jumper. I don't scoff; I don't have to. I do send an incredulous glare at him out of the corner of my eye, and I hear him choke on a chuckle. "I'll explain later," he whispers.

I edge over—

"Slower," Drogan cautions, and I pretend I'm a freaking chameleon, or a stick bug, or any of the things I've seen move super, super *slowly.* My heart's racing like a cheetah, but my body catches on like it's—ha, ha—programmed for this.

Oh, hell. *Thanks evil-scientist team.* At this speed, using this pre-programmed method, surprisingly, the bug-snake-saur doesn't see me.

After everyone scattered, we found a path that cuts through the underbrush, and I was happy pretending that it was made by a species of adorable, harmless deer or maybe bunnies. Little ones. Something—*anything*—vegetarian.

It's kind of getting harder and harder to believe as we encounter yet another bug-a-saur. When they're not shrieking, they're so quiet they manage to get almost on top of us before we realize it. This one puts its head down, doing a frighteningly accurate rendition of 'bloodhound finds trail,' going right to the spot I'd been standing.

It moos.

That's the other strange thing. The last few have made that noise right before they grow very, very agitated. The globular red things emerging from its back pulse even brighter.

Drogan encourages me to get farther away from it. Stay and be found, or amscray and be found.

I don't like this game.

We could shoot them, but handguns are no match for aliens; we found that out early on. It isn't a waste per se, because we survived the encounters unharmed, but we're low on ammo to the extreme now. With the light of dawn making its way through the trees, at least our run-ins with them are happening less and less and the last few didn't even try to attack. Maybe they're tired. It'd be nice if they're not in any way diurnal. That can take effect any time; they can go curl up in their caves of evil or wherever they call home.

Please.

The breath I just took freezes in my lungs when the creature swings its head in my direction. They don't have eyes, yet we've witnessed their accuracy in peeling human beings right off their feet—and sure, maybe it hunts by smell, but I'm not much of a betting woman, so I'm not holding stock on it *not* seeing me.

Except it doesn't.

I look down at myself... and I don't see me either.

"Shhh," I feel more than hear Drogan breathe. "Tell you in a second."

Even my ugly shoes have gone camouflage. My self-cleaning, government-contracted suit? It's got the staying power of a bad penny, because it's still here.

I get a flash memory of a lab tech's face as they called out, *"Nonreactive with fluorescence."*

I hadn't known what they were referring to then.

I look down at my arms. Where my arms should be.

I do now.

I bring my hand up to my face—and I watch leaves dapple across skin, like observing a water ripple when you disrupt it with a pebble.

I'm camo.

They made *me* camouflage.

"I didn't know if it'd work," Drogan says, and his tone is all awe. "It's supposed to activate when you have a need for stealth, but I'd only ever seen it when they forced it in the lab."

I creep to my goal—that'd be *off this path*—keeping my pace slow enough that it looks like the ground is merely being windswept. What it is, is my skin pattern reforming to match our surroundings. I just have to give it time to... do it however it's doing it.

Drogan moves to the opposite side of the trail, also slowly, but without the benefit of skin that's been scientifically altered. I know what he's thinking: if the shrieker wants a meal, I'll have the chance to run because he's going to try to buy me the time.

Using himself.

I don't put my hand on my stomach, but once again, I'm mighty aware of the tiny life I'm carrying.

The shrieker tears up the ground with its rearmost set of back legs, kicking up the vegetation way too close to be comfortable, until all of a sudden, it shuffles past with its head low, thrashing its tail in what looks like a pretty good fit.

I stare after it. "You know how in the books and movies the stranded couple befriends and tames the wild beast?"

Drogan gives me the world's most horrified look. "Fuck. *No.*"

"I didn't say I wanted to." I wave away his overreaction—then I try not to melt when he carefully extracts a twig from my hair. *Aww.* "I was just making conversation, sheesh."

"Mmhmm. You adopted all the strays, didn't you?"

I pivot on my heel. "I'm not going to answer that."

He snorts.

We rejoin the path, still hoping that eventually it will lead to water, a thing we are becoming quite desperate for.

I look up to see Drogan already watching me. He's starting to look (more) worried. I distract him with a question. "When they'd strip me for experiments, I saw them holding up fabric swatches against my skin. I thought I was high on drugs."

"You were."

I roll my eyes at him and watch him grin before he continues. "But you weren't wrong. Your clothes should change as long as they aren't neon."

"How does that work?"

"You know as well as I do that every answer starts with 'Nanotech,' so who fucking knows. Are the grape-things helping at all?"

"Some," I hedge.

"So, *no.*"

I give him a weak smile.

"Have some more," he says as he shoves his handful at me.

Sometime in the night, we came across a giant leaf, with a massive pile of fruit sitting on top of it. It looked like it was gift wrapped for us. Obviously, food doesn't collect itself; someone else must have come through, but we scouted a bit, yet found no sign of anyone else. For all we knew... maybe something had eaten *them.*

We took some grapes.

I push his hand back towards him. "I'm good."

He winces. "Intestinal... problems?"

"Doesn't a hypermetabolism mean it'd be hard for anything to trip up my system?"

He frowns. "Fuck if I know. You were a lab rat not meant to be released into the wild."

"Thanks."

He nods puckishly. I raise him an eyebrow.

I grab his hand as he tries to force it at me again. "You need to eat too. You're the stronger of the two of us and you need to stay that way."

His eyes drop to my stomach, and *that* gets me. Without further argument, I take his alien-grapes and shovel them into my mouth. *I'm starving.* He's already worried, and it's not like he can just pull over at the next fast food joint. Him having to watch me starve to death is bad enough; I don't want him to be tortured before it happens, and me telling him how bad the hunger pangs are will torture him—I can see it as he watches me consume every last bit of fruit.

I can almost feel the food disappear as it hits my stomach. I'm still so famished I don't trust my eyes not to be playing tricks on me when something massive *shifts.*

I peer at the spot I saw movement, and notice something else; *I've seen this thing before.* This *same* thing. "Ryan... did that tree move?"

His fingers slide along my arm; he likes me calling him by his first name. He slowly scans the tree line with me as I point to the tree stump-creature. "Right there. It stopped moving." I glance over my shoulder to see he's way off, so I reach up and guide his chin so that his field of vision matches mine. "The topiary art *right there*—and with the way things have gone in this place so far, it can probably kill us."

"Cheery thought," he agrees easily. "That's the spirit."

"*'How neat, nice dragon.'* That better?"

He frowns. "What makes you call it a dragon?"

"See those things along the sides? Looks like folded wings, right? There is the long neck—"

"That's another tree."

"Is not. And that's the head—see the spikes, like horns?"

"You mean the tree branches?"

I let my hand drop. "So literal! Why can't you agree that it's a living thing?"

He looks unimpressed. "Maybe because it's just a dead tree."

I shake my head at him. "Cloud gazing with you must be fun times."

"Staring at an accumulation of frozen water molecules while you ascribe fantasy animal shapes to them? Sure is."

I wave his tiny, sad, no-imagination scenario away and lay it out. "Okay, well, the dragon topiary is following us—wipe that look off your face. I am telling you: I'm not crazy."

His eyes dance teasingly. "Says every crazy woman..."

We resume walking, mindful to keep our squabbling at a low enough level that predators won't be attracted.

Attracted. He's a bit of an ass, but the more time I get to spend with him, the more I like the man that's arguing with me. I'm filthy, Drogan's once-pristine uniform looks like it took a major beating, yet I still want to jump him. For now, I imagine all the dirty scenarios we could play out as I hope we can find a spot to rest at. I'm starting to feel a little sex-starved.

And as if by magic, our path widens and our field of vision opens; there aren't thousands of trees right in our face for as far as we can see.

It's a peaceful-looking clearing. And creepily enough, right in front of us is another big leaf, with a pile of food on it. Nuts of a sort, it looks like. They're poisoned. They have to be. And the poisoners went too far, thinking that we'd be lulled into complacency after we didn't die the first time—

Drogan reaches for them.

"Hold up there, Hansel! Aren't you worried about this?"

He squints. "The part where we crash landed and we're going to die out here if we don't drink and eat and *if* the animals hunting us don't get us first, or the part where we see food, and we leave it because we're scared something wants to eat us if only they could lure us far enough away from home?"

I push him but he doesn't topple over and the poor man can't tell when he's being insulted because he's grinning like the fool he is. I scoop up the food, preparing to go down with my belly full at least.

We find that we can pop out the edible soft part easily, which is good since we're kind of lacking all supplies and amenities out here. "We're going to get thirsty."

"We're already thirsty. And... Preta?"

I look to where he's pointing.

Giant grooves weave over dirt in pretty but alarming patterns. *What* made them? What do they mean? They lead to another leaf. But on this one, there are half-shells holding *water.*

CHAPTER 7

PETRICHOR

IF WE CAPTURE THIS female, is it still considered poaching? We left our territory to investigate the thing that fell from the sky, and found *females*. We haven't seen females in literal ages. Do the old customs and rules even apply? We don't know who defends this area any longer, but if we did, we'd make an offer of a fair trade for this one. Of all the females that have arrived, she needs males the most; she is in the poorest condition. We've spied her husbandman attempting to obtain rations, but it isn't enough to sustain her; she's wilting right before our eyes.

I'm not surprised they have ignored our note in the dust. We knew it'd be unlikely they'd be able to read our language, but Maceous had hoped.

They do accept our offer of food and drink though, which is promising. They give a cursory look around for us but neither the female nor her husbandman call out for us to join them.

Instead, once she has finished drinking and eating, the female rallies enough to boldly initiate a feeding, and *finally*, her husbandman seems interested in providing for her.

He backs her to Maceous' smooth-barked foreleg.

We stare down at them in shock.

"Are you inviting us to join?" Mace wonders hopefully.

Her voice shakes with repressed laughter when she asks, "Yoor goeeng too fuhk mee agannst eh tuhree?"

She isn't responding to Maceous, but to her husbandman.

He subdues her with a playful hand over her mouth. "Shuht uhp, en eye'll geht yoo awf agannst eh tuhree, woomahn."

He keeps his hand over her mouth to maintain silence, and his unease when he glances around is palpable, wise, and understandable. I'm sure I'm not alone in feeling compelled to share our intentions, and make him a tribe-joining offer simply so he can have peace of mind in this moment.

Yet I say nothing. None of us interrupts as he returns his attention to her, his hand cupping between her legs. It appears as if he possesses plenty of pollen, as he rapidly brings her to peak, and yet—

"What is the knothead doing?" Bortammos whispers beside me.

The husbandman takes a step *back* from her instead of feeding her.

"She is failing to thrive! Can't he see he's starving her?"

I shake my head, confounded. "Maybe he's young. Maybe she's not yet a full scion and without her family's permission he doesn't feel *welcome.*"

She tilts her head up, looking in our direction. We fall silent, waiting politely for her to call out to us. They speak a stranger's tongue; that's not unexpected. She can still call for us if she is interested. That is one of the ways; the other two would be her tribe accepting a trade, or least desirable—we poach her.

I'm hopeful that she is going to choose the most preferable option, until her husbandman distracts her attention from us. "Noww yoor woohred ahbowt teh tuhrees ahgann?"

"Weer maykeeng sohm aneemahls vehree uhpset. Kant yoo heer tem? Leeson. Eye thawt eye herd ah wuhrd."

"Trahnslayter leerns, 'membr? Yoor prahblahblee leerneeng spaysuh sqkwerrl."

"Whut eef eets uhn aleeann mowntayn lyuhn? Yoo dohnt noh!"

When they begin bickering, we resume our conversation. Bortammos slants me a look. "He doesn't appear so young. If I were a sapling I would have fed that female. He must be soddish."

The husbandman in question seems to be growing excited at her torrent of words as they squabble and even goes so far as to clasp her and bite her neck.

Instead of struggling, she wraps all her limbs around him and relaxes.

"He subdues her with his teeth like an animal?"

"Interesting."

Yet he pulls back *again*. He looks around.

Mace peers around with him. "He's worried about an attack." He attempts to sniff his foreleg without bringing his head any further down. "What he needs is the protection of a group."

"Yet they've left theirs," I muse.

"Let's approach him. We can make an appeal to join our tribes."

I *want* to make this appeal. Caution holds me back. Uninterested females run. This one doesn't look strong enough for a chase, and her male may be physically better off, but his exhaustion is apparent. "Let them rest. We can watch over them, give them until night's fall. We can bring them more tapriklut to keep the *Ak'rena* from shrieking over them. She seemed to tolerate the taste."

Mace bares his teeth. "By night's fall she could succumb to starvation. *Look* at her."

I tip my head. "Rush her now and she'll push herself until she's dead." As if to illustrate my point, instead of resting as she so desperately should be, she's pacing with her husbandman as sounds begin to disturb them.

"I believe we're about to see the landowner tribe make an appearance," Mace says. He sounds as discouraged as I'm sure we all feel. We had worked to make this end of the clearing as inviting as possible, adding warm sandy soil perfect for lighting a fire, we'd even provided the tinder and wood, and if our heartstones should happen to be arranged in such a way that the female might notice them, and might even be coaxed to blood them...

We had hoped. But she hasn't so much as glanced down yet, and now with her tribe's arrival, she might not be allowed to blood us even if she suddenly decided to.

Interestingly, it's the husbandman that backs her to the sandy area, and he nudges her to stand right over our heartstones, even going so far as to join her on top of them.

I glance to the other two and see we're all in agreement: this seems like a positive sign.

That is, until all underworld breaks loose.

CHAPTER 8

PRETA

EVEN THE SPACE SQUIRRELS have gone quiet as we wait to see what's snapping twigs and crushing leaves.

Other *humans* materialize from the trees.

Somehow, it's no less threatening to be hunted by people than it is creatures. With the creatures, at least it's not personal. "Any chance these guards are your friends?"

"Negative."

"The boss-guards weren't your friends, the asshole-guard wasn't your friend, the hur-hur *'I'll take her to solitary'* guard wasn't your friend. Stars above, man—did you *have* any friends?"

He spares me a look.

"Oh."

He turns his attention back to the group advancing on us.

"I can't feel it," I whisper.

"Can't feel what?" His fingers sweep down my back, reaching into the pocket of my suit for the handgun tucked there. Quickly, I snake my hand around his hips, and go for the gun in his holster. From this distance, it must look enough like we're hugging, because nobody shoots us for moving.

"I don't have my super powers," I explain, and one of the assholes in front of us is close enough to hear me, and he laughs—a short, surprised sound that seems magnified in the clearing's quiet. Guess he thinks I've gone crazy. I risk a haughty look at Drogan. *Seems that's going around.*

He rolls his eyes at me before we both swing our gazes back to the guy who laughed. This dude could almost be forgiven for thinking that an inmate that survives the *Concord* Treatment is going to be screwed up, but he's not a good guy, so who's going to be in a forgiving mood? Judging by the way he and his friends are eyeing us, we sure as heck won't be.

"I don't care if a bitch is crazy in the head, it don't change her snatch," the chuckler informs us.

His standards are charming. Truly.

"Preta," Drogan says, and in his tone I hear both warning, and regret, and it makes the hairs on the back of my neck stand straight up. "I'm sorry."

I *do not* like the way he says this.

"Do you see the antlers on these stags?"

Just like that, my wiring is back online. The group in front of us pauses, confusion plain on their faces as they glance around, looking for said stags.

I take out three in rapid succession, Drogan takes out another, and as if we choreographed it, we swing to fire on the last two. The sound of strikers hitting nothing but chamber is about as terrifying as it can get when the opposition has you, quite literally, in their sights. We could have cleared this field by now if we'd had the bullets.

A bellow of terrifying proportions splits the air. It's different from the shrieker call, this one so deep the ground under our feet shakes, and it makes everyone hesitate.

I whip my now-useless handgun at them.

I was never good at throwing—well, not good at aiming either, really, but it strikes my target smack in the forehead and he goes down.

But it's too little, too late. The last man aims, just before something rushes him from the trees.

Drogan's already leaping to tackle me, twisting us, and I think his plan was for him *not* to land on me. On account of a bullet grazing his leg, he isn't able to execute it as smoothly as he planned. I end up under him, and he is *heavy*. I didn't know I should have counted myself lucky we always banged against a wall—this brute is *crushing* me. My face smashes into a rock, making my eyes water and my nose bleed.

When his body lifts off of me with a pained shout, I roll over, my hand going to my nose now that his weight isn't pinning my limbs in place, and I ask, "Are you okay..."

I hadn't been sure what was attacking the last shooter, and with Drogan going full bodyguard on me, I hadn't had the millisecond to worry about it yet.

That millisecond opening is happening right now.

Suspended above me is Drogan, and he's being held aloft by a very alive dragon-tree. Twisting branches, clinging plant life, and *now* I see the eyes; how did we miss these before? They project light like they've got halogen lamps in their sockets. But the surface is shiny and glistens like a normal eye. *A living tree-creature.*

Movement has me panning my gaze around to see that there are *three* of them.

One of them holds his foot—*his hand?*—up in front of me, spreading his claws. I scramble to my feet, my mind a jumble of useless commands in this instance. There is *no* protocol for *this*.

I don't see the tree-dragon's other hand until it scoops me up from behind.

CHAPTER 9

PRETA

I'M COLD. INSIDE, and out. Drogan said I'd be practical, and despite the fact that I feel like a tundra chip has replaced the heart in my chest, my mind is giving me orders. The targets are dead, so I've been released from the killer sequence and I've been supplied with the next essential task: *assess teammate condition, and immediately find food source.*

Whoever wrote this program spent way too much time with computers and not enough time with loved ones. It's a bit of a relief that I am *scared* for Drogan, and although I feel like the old me would have been panicking right now, panicking about arteries, and infection, and the lack of supplies to prevent infection—I have a handle on myself. I don't want to be the old panicky me, but I'm relieved I'm not entirely unfeeling.

I'd take the food suggestion in a heartbeat though. Because *starving.*

Just before he cups me in his massive palms, the creature rakes his claws along the ground and picks up... a rock?

Some birds swallow stones to help them break down food in their gullets. What do dragons (!) *made of trees* (!!) do?

I don't know yet, but I do know it's *real,* it *is* alive, and it *picked! Me! Up!*

Air rushes over me as its wings flick open and slam down, launching us into the air.

My heart settles down a little when I see that Drogan is being carried by the biggest tree-dragon... not that this is a great thing, but leaving him lying in the dirt, wounded, prey for anything, sounds worse than... whatever is about to happen to us—at least we'll be together.

Not 'at least he won't be alone,' but an emphatic 'we'll be *together*.' I'd like to think that's the romantic side of me wanting to keep us tight, but I'm more afraid it's my programming attempting to salvage its unit.

Images flit in my mind; more sequences—for escape this time—it feels like my brain is shouting all sorts of commands at me. For instance, one command scenario involves the rock this dragon has with us, but I immediately reject the idea that I use it as a weapon because this behemoth plummeting out of the sky while he's clutching me is not a good play.

Movement has me chancing a look up at a GIANT eye. *"Ahhh!"*

Its head rears back, which changes its momentum which means I end up slamming against its opposite half-cupped finger. Its nose is suddenly against me, nudging. "Hey! Quit it! You're going to push me off!"

It brings its other hand around me though, so that I'd have to stand up and jump if I wanted out now—which I do not. The ground is currently far, far below us. I'm bathed in hot breath, and I cough, feeling like I've just opened the door on a car that's been baking over summer-heated asphalt. I shove at the nose, and I have to catch myself when it immediately moves away from the pressure of my hand. "Thanks," I gasp.

Its head tilts. *"Keilmort'baan din."*

My translator pushes, "Welcome."

I knew it! This—*this!*—is the source of the 'space squirrel' chatter Drogan was giving me crap about! I *did* hear alien creatures talking and my translator *is* learning! It's supposed to be able to teach itself any language. It's been learning tree-dragon!

I look at the thing—as much of its body as I can see—its massive face, the thickness of its neck, and the expanse of its chest are so big, I *can't* see around it. In front of me though, it looks like it's made up of braided vines and moss. It has a head shield like a Triceratops, but made of branches. This thing is entirely made of various types of plant life, and it reminds me of terrarium art. Just on a way, way bigger scale.

I scoot forward on my knees, squinting at its shoulder. There's a bird nest on it. There's a bird *in* it.

The poor thing looks kind of freaked out, and I wonder if its mate is going to be looking from tree to tree, unable to find home, grass bits or night crawler worms dropping from its little beak when it shouts in bird, "WHAT THE HELL?!"

I shake my head—then just as quickly, I put a hand up to my temple. I'm starting to feel dizzy, something I've been fighting off and on for hours, but the crummy excuses for food I've been able to consume at least kept the worst of that at bay. My head is also starting to pound, and for now, with a daredevil skydive off this dragon's hands not looking like my best option just yet, I settle for closing my eyes, and hunkering down on his palm.

CHAPTER 10

PETRICHOR

I'M LOSING HER. "DO not die," I order, even though I know she can't understand me. Her eyes pop open, and my heartstone flares next to her, which makes her sit up. This is good. She's still responsive despite the stresses placed on her by fear and the extreme effects of hunger.

Dimly registering the caress of the Sonhadra sky on my wings, I skirt the unfinished city, our Ruler's pride and joy once, and descend to our hometree. I'm gentle with her as I shift to my two-legged form; I don't want to drop my azibo.

My azibo. *I have an azibo.*

I look much like her now, though she is soft-skinned, whereas my skin is like packed loam, and might grow the occasional creeping vine and twisting twig. Sharing a similar appearance in shape does not comfort her, however.

She begins to struggle, and to counter it, I lock my arm around her, and carefully reach up to my shoulder to transfer the bird's nest to a nearby tree before it gets dislodged by her thrashing. I tug up a few small shrubs and drop them in front of it to act as a windblock should the weather take a turn in the night.

In the circle of my arms, my azibo falls still, which takes my attention off of nest cozying in order to access her condition.

She's looking at the bird.

I turn back to it too, but it seems fine. "Your mate will find you," I tell it and very carefully stroke my finger over its silky-feathered head.

My azibo makes a small noise, her eyes darting to mine when I look down at her in question. Slowly, I take her hand and bring it up so she too can pet the bird. Her fingers stay limp, her head turning to me in question until I demonstrate, and verbally explain, how carefully she should move.

She brings her forehead forward and widens her eyes, her strips of brow turf rising straight up. I get the sense that she knows *how* to pet a bird—she simply wasn't certain of my intention. I laugh. "My apologies."

Tentatively, she takes over, and when she's done, the bird seems confused about being touched by a stranger, but my azibo's anxiety about *me* is nearly extinguished.

I stare down at her. If petting small animals is reassuring, I can take her to meet all sorts; I begin to consider who best to introduce her to, and which ones have litters with young, because babies of all kinds are a joy to behold. My azibo shifts and the boniness of the hip against my stomach makes me wince for her. *Forget introductions*—feeding first. I thought I'd wait for her husbandman to arrive, but she needs replenishing as quickly as possible.

"Pretty," she says as I open the intricately-woven door at the base of our hometree. I ponder her expression—her word, not only her face—relieved that I am now able to understand her speech because she blooded me when she was injured on my heartstone. I don't know about the other valos in the land, but the Kahav gain their azibo's speech immediately, as a gift from our Ruler, who wanted our pairings successful.

After all, more families meant more workers.

She continues to appreciate the beauty of her new surroundings as I swiftly carry her through the maze of tunnels that make up our warren. Throughout this, she remains relaxed against me, trusting.

I almost breathe a sigh of relief, but when we arrive at my bed, I feel as if I'm very suddenly holding onto warm stone. Her trusting, relaxed manner has disappeared along with her interest in her surroundings. She's focused on me now, and from where I grip it in my hand, I spy my heartstone glowing like chastising fire in reaction to the betrayal she's feeling.

I set her down carefully, and I want to be relieved that she doesn't attempt escape, but seeing her resignation is no better a sight. Discontent fills my chest as I slowly and gently begin to work her odd coverings loose.

I stop when I see her skin begin to change pattern. I witnessed this when one of the land beasts of the area was stalking her. Like most beings that can conceal themselves into the background, they most often display this trait when they feel threatened or frightened.

I take her hand, and am further saddened when she doesn't so much as try to fight me. I can see that she is feeling weak and in this it's almost as if I can read her thoughts; resistance is futile, and *assault* is inevitable.

I want to point out many things, starting with the fact that this must be done now because her husbandman did not feed her as he should have. Yet, casting blame on another husbandman seems like a terrible method of easing her misgivings—let alone the fact that doing so would be an inauspicious start in the extreme. "You need to feed," I try to explain.

Unfortunately, blooding my heartstone does not make it so that *she* can understand *me*. This was a common enough problem in the days when females were brought from other tribes. There would be a period of courting, in which we would learn about each other's language and cultures, and it is unfortunate that we do not possess this luxury of time due to her condition.

I'm still uneasy and wondering how to explain when, with a startling swiftness, she returns to her natural coloration.

When she gives me a dull look and tugs on her hand, I let her go. She begins to remove her coverings herself, starting with her feet. I move back to give her more room. Her stoicism is admirable, but it is painful that she has to exercise it at all. I feel her unhappiness like sour notes from a still-green piper flute. This is all wrong.

"Here," I bring my heartstone to her lips. "At least we can complete this part properly."

I've seen her eyes dance playfully. I've seen her eyes turn heated with lust for her husbandman. I've seen her eyes go fierce before a battle.

Now the summer-warmed brown has turned muddy, and all of her has lost a luster. She's *tolerating* this, not welcoming it—*me*. It's turning our ceremony into something forced, and ugly, and without prolonging what should have been a joyous joining, I press my stone to her lips.

She doesn't react except to part them as if she's ready to take it into her mouth. With growing incertitude, I pull it back, and plug it into my chest.

A little bit of spark comes back to her person as great vines of ivy bloom and weave, and unravel across my skin, tiny crimson and vermilion flowers budding and unfurling right before her stunned eyes.

By her shock, she's never blooded a Kahav before—this much is obvious. I don't know what her husbandman's ceremony involves, but I know many valo have a heartstone that comes alive for their azibo.

Azibo.

I have an azibo.

I've dreamed of this day for so long. I've imagined how it would happen, and how beautiful it would be to twine together. To provide for her. Wanting just this one small aspect to match the scene I've often relished in my head, I lean in to press a kiss to her forehead.

She tips up her face in the last moment, and our lips touch instead.

CHAPTER 11

PRETA

PRACTICAL. THAT'S what Drogan said my programming was at its base. It's sure defaulted to practicality now. I've never been more aware of my options: I can fight and lose to an alien that, in his tree-dragon form, has teeth longer than my forearm—or I can just give him what he wants, and hope he's pleased enough he won't hurt me, yet *not* have so much fun that he wants multiple sessions.

I don't need to gather courage, or anything. I feel like I'm a spectator as I numbly consider this towering male specimen that looks sort of human now. He's got moss for hair and eyebrows, and his skin has areas that look like grit, with raised parts that aren't stone, but aren't skin either.

He smells great. That shouldn't matter at all, but I guess it's just a nice bonus not to be taken advantage of by an alien that oozes and stinks like a urinal cake; little bits of luck can't be taken for granted. I breathe out and look up at the ceiling.

Submit. He's an alien creature and it's obvious he's horny. This is the smart play—I'm not strong enough to stop him—I can be raped or I can help myself along, make him happy, and hope I get a chance to slip away. Really, it could be worse; this guy could have shifted into a human-ish thing back there and thrown me down right in front of Drogan, but he didn't, and a soft bed underground seems like a nice gesture by comparison. I hope the other two bring Drogan to the same tunnels and if I do get to escape, I can find him and we can both make it out of here alive.

With a gunshot wound?

Between my dad and Charlie, I know gunshots spell infection and downtime. It's not like the movies where the hero gets to run around and take bullets like tickles.

Don't borrow trouble, just complete this and live to tackle the next crises. "All you have to do is have sex with the horny alien, Preta. No big deal. Man up!"

He stops moving.

So do I. My stomach drops as I lift my eyes and see dark emotion flash across his face. It seems impossible that he'd have known what I was saying, and yet thirty seconds ago, lying under a man who had just shifted from a dragon made out of a tree would have sounded a little more unlikely, so...

Male pride can be a dangerous thing to bruise. *Seduce,* my mind orders me, and this time, my words stay in my head and away from my mouth, thankfully. "Do you understand me?"

His face doesn't change, yet I can swear he recognizes what I'm saying—I have got to be more careful. I clear my throat. "Talk to me," I manage, and despite my throat feeling tight, my voice comes out normal. Calm. Like I lie back and let it happen every day. "My translator learns," I explain as I tap my ear.

Instead, he puts his hand on my crotch and squeezes.

CHAPTER 12

PETRICHOR

GAZE ON HER, I SPEAK. "You're beautiful, even spindly as you are."
I draw the backs of my fingers down her face, and watch her eyes go
hooded. Not from passion, I realize; she's attempting to hide her emotions from me. I suppose this is effective, as I can't tell what she's feeling, but I can guess. I try to put her at ease. With my other hand at the
apex of her thighs, I apply prevernal pollen to prepare her. The pollen-
giving is yet another gift created by our Ruler, who had grand desires
for our tribe's successful matings.

It relaxes her even as it stimulates; her body bucks and her eyes
go wide. She's shocked. This is odd; I witnessed that her husbandman
could do this much for her.

Has he never fully *fed* her? Perhaps they were being driven too hard
by the hostile group.

I feel her body pull more pollen from me than I expect. I suppose I
shouldn't be surprised; perhaps her kind requires more, or perhaps it is
because we don't know each other well, and she is consciously control-
ling the amount because her body requires more to be prepared.

I am grateful her nose is no longer bleeding, though the blood remains, and has dried to her skin. Next to the bed is a pitcher of water,
and a basin and rag. She lets me clean her as best as I'm able, my movements efficient, and when I'm done, I gently pat her dry with a spare
cloth. My movements are slower now, and I'm examining the extent of
her thinness. Absently, I stroke my thumbs along the too-prominent
collarbone, gliding a light touch up her throat, and instantly, I feel her
relax beneath me.

"Ryan?"

"He's being treated," I assure her.

Her brow turfs come together, and her pupils are very large and her eyes aren't quite focused on me when she asks again, "Ryan?"

Odd. *Oh...* she's acting *pollenlogged!* She took too much. It will wear off, but in the meantime, she might experience some confusion, but she will definitely be prepared for a feeding. I try again. "...I promise you they're helping him. Right now, you require a feeding."

Her arm comes up, bumping the one I have at her neck, and my hand slips, landing against the juncture of her jaw and throat.

She settles instantly.

It's the grip; she wants to be gripped. This must be what her Ryan does for her when they come together. I try to think back on when she was attempting to initiate a feeding with her husbandman up against Mace's leg; he had a hold on her face, and now that I concentrate, I think he did slide his other hand to her throat for a time too.

She... likes to be held this way. I suppose that's not so very strange. I have seen female animals of all sorts that respond to their necks being restrained during mating—why not some valo tribes? It makes enough sense that I keep my hand there a moment, watching to see if she becomes distressed, and when she only relaxes further, I'm almost certain this is what it must be.

Touching her like this, I can feel her exhaustion, her *depletion,* and I've already been extremely worried for her condition, feeling some of what she feels only adds urgency: *she must be fed immediately.* With my free hand, I struggle to remove the last of her strange coverings. They don't simply part at her thighs, or lift away, or anything normal. She's as closed up as a bloom in the dark. I begin to wonder if she needs to be coaxed out of them, and learn this is so when my fumbling goes on long enough that she begins to attack at them herself. I watch in fascination as she reveals her outer layer possesses many teeth, and she drags a strange fastener across them to encourage them to open. I try to test this by tugging them in reverse, my ears pricking as I hear an odd *zzzzip!* It is unlike any hiss I've ever heard before, but before I can examine this further, she bats my hands away in order to complete her shed.

It's an odd thing, what she wears. Most females are drab, and muted in color. Not so with my azibo. Her skin is the russet shade of washed sand, and her covering is garishly bright, either to serve as a warning or an attractant, I'm uncertain which. I can't say I find it alluring; intriguing yes, but it isn't... whatever she dyed it with to reach this hue must be quite deadly as you rarely see anything so bright unless it's near to killing you. It's the way of the forest. The meek and mild hide, while the aggressive and wild will poison, attack, or eat you.

I look down into her face, drawn again to the blacks of her pupils, each surrounded with a tiny rim of color. She's starved and done with waiting. She's fully succumbed to the pollen and I'm relieved beyond measure, because it was killing us to watch her wither away. It doesn't matter if she's never been fed or if she's simply gone too long without a proper feeding—she is safe here, and we will take care of her from now on. Flushed cheeks, writhing against my palm as I try to replace it over the new, soft, white inner layer covering that she has revealed—she dislodges my hand when I try to touch this, and rips the layer off; she's ravenous and won't be denied.

This is understandable; she knows how badly she needs nourishment.

She proves this when her hand moves from where she was gripping my arm, to shove aside my loincloth and clutch at my rootstem. Hissing, I try to catch her; I can see the tendrils starting to grow and I'm not even inside her yet. "Wait," I warn, but she's beyond the ability to listen. I might be the first Kahav that she has ever been fed by, but her instinct has been *triggered.* She uses my base to drag my body to hers, and guides me into her warm, welcoming slit.

"Sunshine above," I gasp, and my hips snap forward. My body hunches over hers as I try to make sense of everything I'm feeling.

She's *not hollow* inside.

She's squeezing heat and fluid encouragement and the shock of it has my rootshaft aching for immediate release. I'm eager to comply; I simply don't know where to plant my tendrils. Carefully, I send them seeking and am not surprised at all to find they've elongated on their own while I was busy being engulfed by her exquisite sensations. Underneath me, she's gasping, clutching at me, and attempting to gyrate her hips upward, which causes my tendrils to shiver inside her and I can't venture to guess what she feels as she writhes in reaction, but if it's half as pleasurable as what I'm feeling, neither one of us may survive this.

I cup my hand over her mound, and run my double thumbs down until I discover her bud hidden at the top of her petals. She makes a startled noise but doesn't deter me as I slowly attempt to bring her pleasure.

To add to her new sensations, my tendrils unfurl inside her, gently sliding between her walls, brushing along her insides, making her squirm beneath me in a dance as old as the soil.

I wait, gritting my teeth against the urge to surge into her as her movements turn into impatient bucks of her hips and she reveals she has sharp edges on her fingers, like surprise thorns on a delicate beauty of a Loess flower. She digs these into me, and I'm shocked that my body responds, my own enjoyment heightening. It is pleasurable for her, as it should be, but I want nothing more than to spill my seed, and it's not time yet. I feed her more prevernal pollen, readying her for implantation.

She is nearly at completion, yet there hasn't been a blossoming, and I'm confused until it dawns on me just why that could be.

Our azibo has been fertilized by another.

Seed will not come forth from me—it can't. I can still feed her though, and as my gaze sweeps down her naked form, I'm appalled anew that she's been reduced to a state where her body has sunken in on itself in malnourished desperation.

If the sensation of the tendrils pleased her, the first hit of nectar drives her wild.

She cries out, and as her knees tighten against my sides, her back arches off of the soft leaves of the bed beneath her. I want to watch her. I want nothing more than to see this, but my vision goes dark as her body calls mine to release more, more-more-*more*. She is *starving*.

She reveals a set of exquisite inner muscles that clamp down and begin to *flutter* and draw out more nectar.

She's going to drain me.

I feel sudden pity for her husbandman. This is why she is in such poor condition—I don't know how long he has been alone, but there is no way a single husbandman can provide enough, and it must have caused him great amounts of worry and guilt.

I tense as I receive an odd, echoing shock; it's from her. One of my tendrils seems particularly interested in the upper wall of her cavern, a fact I find curious because it's driving her absolutely *mindless*. I feel moisture gathering at our joining; it is increasing her saturation level to a delightful degree. It is affecting her so strongly that I'm sharing in her sensations, and long ago, this was the mark of a good coupling. I clutch at her hip and her shoulder, wondering what more I should do to topple her over this peak she is experiencing when she bows her back off of the bed and begins to seize in obvious pleasure. "Drogan!" she cries out in ecstasy. Her limbs shudder and she writhes and her body tightens, and tightens—

My heartstone speaks no translation for her cry, but I feel her sudden rush of affection and, almost giddy from it, I proudly repeat her exclamation, roaring, *"DROGAN!"*

I hear a male's shout, and dimly, all I can register is that it's not mine.

As her eyes drift shut, body drowsy from the nectar my root is pumping, feeding into her, I watch her skin take on a richer tone.

She begins to look sun-kissed right before my eyes, and it shouldn't be possible but she becomes more glorious.

My hand manages to brush reassuringly along the outside of her thigh once before I put everything into the concentration it takes not to collapse on top of her in exhaustion.

CHAPTER 13

PETRICHOR

THE HOLLOWS ON HER body fill out as they should, and I talk softly to her—more in an attempt to keep myself awake than to fill the quiet. I want her to be able to rest, but I can also see that even slipping into unconsciousness, she is liking the sound of my voice, and it warms me to see her relax even further when I drop down on my elbows so that our chests touch, and she can feel everything I'm saying to her too.

Feel everything. Her stomach!

I roll off of her immediately, then laugh at myself. At this stage, the Sproutling will be exactly that, a tiny sprout, and thankfully, it and its mother will be fine despite my cloddish inattention. It isn't as if I'm not familiar with young; a constant circle of life is teeming within the Salachar forest that the Kahav call home.

The Kahav. There are only three of us still lifegreen. I let my eyes climb up my azibo's now beautifully curved body, and think, *Now there are four.* My hand finds her stomach, and in sleep, her hands slowly move to cover mine. *Five.*

Her husbandman makes six.

We've doubled our number thanks to them. And someday, she might bear Ammos', or Maceous', or my own Sproutlings, and the Kahav will flourish once more.

I roll my eyes skyward and mutter, "May the Ruler never return." Something the Ruler did killed off all the females. Like an early frost, they succumbed overnight. It was devastating. Woven males followed, wilting after their females.

The memories make me feel even more depleted, and my fingers tremble as I reach to pluck the most beautiful bloom from where it is growing over my heartstone. I gently sweep her hair back from her face, and tuck it behind her ear.

I doze next to her for a time, but I know her husbandman will want to be assured of her renewed condition, so I struggle to rise without disturbing her. Exhausted, I stumble out of the room, and go in search of the others. Upon reaching them, I manage the shaky announcement, "She has a Sproutling."

Maceous looks unimpressed. "We could have told you that."

Archly I challenge, "And you would know this how?"

"Because it pulls at us."

"You're not woven to her," I say in consternation, my head feeling thick and my thoughts sluggish.

"We are to *him*," Bortammos says pointedly. "His leg bled on our heartstones." I turn around, and there is our new husbandman, mouth stuffed with gaius-gum. It will help control the amount of pain he is obviously experiencing, which is evidenced in the way he is clutching the injury site from the strange weapon the warring tribesman attacked him with. Gaius-gum will also keep his jaws stuck fast, keep him from calling out and alarming her, which from the sound of his muffled snarling, he might attempt to do.

I shuffle in his direction. To the others, I pose a question. "Why don't I sense the Sproutling?"

Ammos removes a terran weed from between his lips. "Hmm. The Sproutling takes after our new tribesman. *Greatly.*"

Pondering what that could mean, and feeling weary in a way I've never experienced, I approach our aggressive new tribesmember. Even injured to the point he's been rendered lame, he's full of fury and indignant rage.

"Husbandman," I start.

"FuCK awff!" he snarls.

Bortammos turns to me, eyes and expression arrayed in a clear wince. "He's issued an aggressive order for you to depart."

"That," I nod slowly, not taking my eyes from the injured man, "I gathered." I can understand him as clearly as I do her, because she blooded me, and the pair shares a language. For the same reason, Ammos and Mace will understand her thanks to her husbandman blooding them. The gaius-gum adds a challenge, however, and I appreciate Ammos' effort to assist. I imagine in the time I spent with our azibo, this new tribesmember offered opportunity aplenty for them to learn his new nuance in speech.

"He has an attitude," Mace offers, his tone dry as soot. "And we knew the first feeding would be taxing, but you look as if the lightest gale could send you crashing down."

I try to nod, but feel as if my balance is interfering with even this. "It is lucky their tribesman is even conscious if he's carried the sole feeding responsibility. She depleted me of nectar," both Mace and Ammos swing me shocked gazes. "I venture he is too and this is why she's in the condition she is. He *can't* feed her." My vision feels like it's furling black at the edges, and I try to blink it away. "Oh. Beware, she doesn't sip pollen. She *sucks*."

I bob my head at their wide-eyed expressions. When the three of us fall silent and focus on her husbandman, his eyes narrow and he puffs up, a feat to behold when he has no fur, or scales, or spines with which to offer such a defensive display.

"Tfry itf, affhoes!"

Ammos replaces his stalk of terran weed and peers at him. "It's strange that there is no translation for this last one. *Affhoes*. I like the sound of it—I just don't know what it means."

"Something vile, I'd imagine," Mace offers.

"I know," Ammos says easily. "It's about time we learned new curse words. It's been ages and everything we say has gone stale."

Yet another reason we found ourselves in our Guardian forms more and more. Everything had gone stale. "What do we do with him?"

Mace stands and *Ryan,* I try to teach myself, begins that odd growling speech again. Mace pays him no mind. "He's worried for the azibo. It should settle him to be reunited with her."

"But he'll wake her—"

"I don't think he will." Mace points to Ryan, then points in the direction of our azibo, trying to put him at ease as to where and why he's about to be moved. They seem to be coming to an uneasy truce before Mace begins to lift him.

Remembering what I have clutched in my hand, I hold the tiny items out to Ammos. "Do you think you can make something in her size?"

Ryan takes one look at what I'm holding, and he loses his grip on sanity.

CHAPTER 14

RYAN

HE HAD HER FUCKING bra and panties! I'm cursing every one of them and their mothers when they haul me into the bedroom of their underground lair, but the breath leaves me when I see Preta, naked, raped unconscious.

Pain slices through my chest and the rage makes it impossible to see her for a moment—snarling at the creatures that are carrying me like the invalid I fucking am, I suck air in through my teeth and try to get my head on straight, and look her over for injuries. What *I* feel in this moment doesn't matter. She—

I stare at her.

"MOTHERF—!" I might be hitting a high note on this one as my leg gets jostled. The asshole setting me down right now wasn't even trying to be an asshole—even hurt, *boiling* with aggression, and yes, fear, I can tell that much—he *tried* to go easy.

And Preta... Her... She looks...

Healthy.

She looks *fed*. Not that greenish just-got-injected-with-serum-and-I'm-about-to-hurl 'fed'—she looks even better now than the day I first saw her. This must be what she looked like before the research team took an interest in her.

Initially, I'd been relieved as hell when I'd gotten the transfer from the men's levels to the women's. I assumed reassignment to their part of the 'hood meant, among other things, that it'd be less dangerous.

For me, it was.

For the women? I did not fucking know women could be so damn evil. My first day there, I broke up a broomstick party. The shit those bitches do to the newbie and weaker inmates is sick. Not that men are any better; it's just that there's this expectation that women are the gentler, fairer sex.

What-fuckin'-ever.

A few hours of their cat-calling me—an event somehow as equally disturbing as when the male inmates did it—and I was of the opinion that there should just about be a prison-wide wipe. Almost *none* of these freaks deserved to live—

I caught sight of Preta.

She didn't see me; she was with two other women. Quiet. No active, harmful activity. Technically, they weren't doing anything interesting at all, and THAT was the part that made them stand out. They were softly laughing, smiling; they looked so normal in their issued garb.

By pure chance, Preta glanced up, and caught me watching. As soon as her eyes met mine, my boots might as well have been locked to the floor; I was stunned—she was so *pretty*. She however, looked away quickly, and whatever she muttered to her pals had them giving me looks so discreet that if I hadn't already been staring so hard, I'd never have noticed they were doing it. She told them not to look—I'm sure of it. She probably said, "The new guard is watching us." I sure was. I kept watching too. She was my job. The rest of them could be damned.

Every shift, I watched her try to buoy her friends, Quinn, Lydia, and Zoya, and watched them comfort her too. I saw a woman who was trying to make the best of her circumstances.

Basically, I creeped on the 'criminal' with a heart of gold and a million-dollar smile.

Not that she ever turned it on me. She tried to ignore me, but I saw her flash it easily at her pals.

Then they took her friends away, and I watched her become needy—not for replacements, she *knew* the other women would never be her friends—but she couldn't help it that her system was jonesing for a unit. It was exactly the outcome they wanted to see from her, their little experiment.

Experiment. That's exactly what she is: lab-made. We're talking crates of serum and a special, chemical-laden, specifically nutritionally designed diet with a friggin' team of medical professionals who were assigned to dole all that out, and monitor and keep her system in order.

How in the hell did *aliens* living in dirt manage this? The smaller of the two chewed up a leaf and *spit* it into my bullet wound for fuck's sake! That's the extent of their med-care abilities!

"Should we leave them?" I hear them asking each other. I am futilely wishing for my guns, my knife, even the shock baton in my hands right now, but part of me grudgingly appreciates that they keep their voices low enough not to bother Preta. Despite whatever they did to her... she doesn't *look* hurt. I resist the urge to flip the weird, fuzzy caterpillar-blanket off of her midsection and see for myself if they...

I swallow, and take careful hold of it to gently tug it over her instead so that she's covered neck to knees. I don't know what happened, but I know for damn sure I don't want her feeling any more vulnerable than she already will be in front of our captors and her possible rapist. *Thinking* it has me glaring at him. For good measure, I spread that look around at all of them and part of me tries to relax because two of them at least are backing away—the ones that were with me. But *not* the one that was alone with her. I bare my teeth at this monkeyballmuncher.

Despite trying to avoid it, Preta rouses a little anyway. Unlike after her visits to the lab, her eyes don't have the drugged look; confused, yes, and even though she doesn't look like a run-over raccoon—something she jokes that she resembles on experiment days—she still looks like she could use sleep. Or maybe that's just me, needing to see her peacefully resting a little longer, so I can assure myself that she's okay. That whatever they did to her, she'll be all right.

"I'm here, Sol," I tell her as I set my thumb to stroking her collarbone, her throat.

She exhales and her eyes droop even further, her entire body relaxing at the sound of my voice and it fucking *kills* me. This sense of security is *false*—I haven't been able to keep her safe. I've even tweaked the roster so that *I* was the one escorting her back and forth to the diabolical doctors—she should *not* trust me, I do not deserve this blind faith.

I brush her hair back from her temple, dislodging a flower that got stuck in it—it's actually kinda pretty so I fit it back behind her ear, trying not to crush it as I clumsily tuck the little stem into her locks, ignoring the excited voices of the aliens as I do it—and for the friggin' millionth time, I think, *I wish we hadn't met like this.* She should never have been in Alpha pod. She didn't belong there, or the crash, and she doesn't deserve this—whatever happened to her *here*, and whatever is going to happen *after* this. She should be back on Earth. If we'd met—

I pull up a little, but I don't stop petting her. It's making the worry lines creasing her forehead almost disappear.

If we'd met before this all happened, I don't know if Preta would have liked me.

I can guarantee I'd have liked her.

I can't shake the belief that she's not a whole lot different now than she was before Alpha pod happened. I asked her once, how she could still smile. Her answer?

"Oh, please. This place is nothing—I used to work in Customer Service."

The memory makes my mouth tip up.

Preta rewired my brain. Prison's changed me too, even if I wasn't technically the one behind bars. I feel like I've grown up and aged ten years in just the few months of that hellhole. As I stare down at her, ignoring that we're being silently watched (what else is new? Aliens instead of cameras, such a fucking step up), I decide that if I'd met Preta before, I'd have recognized something this fucking special, and I've had gotten my shit together for her. I know she thinks she was just a fuck for me, but that wasn't it. Not for me. And somewhere inside her, she does trust me. We really hit it off, and we have something, chemistry.

Or it's her programming.

Brutally, I squelch the voice. I don't want to hear it.

Needing to escape the turn my thoughts are trying to take, I drag my eyes away from her, putting a halt on the puppy-dog stare I can't seem to quit whenever I get in her vicinity. I look at our surroundings, still ignoring the assholes watching us. The ceiling is the underside of a tree. Everything, the walls, the floor—dirt, because we're in damn tunnel within a mess of tunnels under the ground. We were airlifted here by garden art come to life—just like she warned me, these freaks are not *dead* trees, and I so desperately need her to be okay so she can give me shit later about exactly how wrong I was—and they flew us to a giant weird-ass tree, and dove through a friggin' hobbit door at the base of it to introduce us to their creepy lair.

A creepy lair that does not look creepy at all right now. It looks warm, safe from whatever the hell creatures are out in the jungle trying to attack us at all hours, and from the quiet, I am going to assume we're the only humans here, which is not all bad since our own kind were only too happy to kill us. Or at least me. I comprehend that they wanted to keep Preta as a plaything.

Fuck.

I relive the fear that she'd be mobbed, and my heartbeat ramps up, along with my fury... and my sense of helplessness. My leg's throbbing intensifies as my blood pressure rises and I have to close my eyes and try to calm myself down. She's... I don't know what happened, but she seems okay. And maybe I can find out. I slit my gaze, struggling for diplomacy as I stare down our captors. Rescuers, if they aren't actually hurting us, but that's to be determined. "What did you do to her?" It's the calmest I've been since before we were set upon by other humans.

I'm actually feeling calmer than I have since we crash landed. Worry notwithstanding, the rest of me thinks we're all good now.

Right.

Just because they haven't torn us apart doesn't mean that everything's good, that they *intend* to leave us unharmed.

"Fed her," one supplies. It's the big one that picked me up from where I was helplessly splayed on the ground, not even able to drag myself to Preta in time to save her—not that I could *do* a damn thing to save her.

Deep breath. *Fucking leg.*

He's also half of the duo that is responsible for my leg wound being rinsed and wrapped up. I'd have been real grateful, if I hadn't known Preta was with the third one, and when she called out my name, I thrashed around like any minute I'd go full superhero and get us out of this.

I drop the pissing contest when I feel her fingers close over mine; I didn't realize I'd moved my hand over hers, but I did, and even in her sleep, she's unintentionally reminding me there's too much to lose. *I can't leave her alone here. I have to hang on. I'll be fine.* I ignore all the clamoring in my head, *sepsis* being my biggest worry. I grip my burning thigh, and glare at all of them. "That all?"

They look confused.

"*What did you* do *to her?* Where are her fucking clothes?" I grit out. Fucking pervs have her underwear like trophies. It makes me feel a little better that it looks like she damn near killed the alien that took them from her. "What are you? What do you want with her? And what is *that* thing on top of her?" I didn't mean to ask this, but it's freaking me out. However, saying the words *on top of her* makes my mind go to what they had to have done to her, and my stomach twists and squeezes so hard I feel like I'm going to barf. My head pounds, so does my leg—

"We are the Kahav," the nurse is the one that answers this time. He has nice hands, I think stupidly, and I hope the one that was in here with Preta was as—

I want to grab at my pounding temples, but to do that, I'd have to take either my hand from my leg or from Preta, and that's not happening. So I just keep staring at the weird trio.

"She is our azibo..." he pauses here, like he's waiting for me to interrupt and tell him she's not their damn *any*thing, "her strange clothing was filthy, and that," he uses all three of his weird fucking fingers to point to the caterpillar, "is keeping her comfortably warm, as you already should have guessed."

His tone has turned into, 'and I think you're being a dickweed about this.' I narrow my eyes at him. "I didn't ask what it was for," I bite out like a prick, but fear keeps trying to get a hold on me and the dread, the knowledge that the one did more to her than just strip her is trying to drag me down and beat me. "I asked what it was."

Not even when I was fighting them to get to Preta did they slip in expression—until now. The one that pulled that sticky shit from my mouth and carried me looks a little fucking affronted, like me questioning this is an insult. "It's a kru-kru skin. Yatavi?"

My little translator? It learns. And it just committed *yatavi* to memory, in *that* tone, as *'happy now, asshole?'* Despite myself, I smile.

As I fought them and cursed them earlier, they spoke to me. My translator did its friggin' job, and I would have started to calm down once I registered that their words were matching their actions: carefully fixing me up, trying to calm down the crazy bastard they had on their hands—but there was the whole 'Preta's getting raped next door' that I was having trouble getting over it enough to relax back and be appreciative. And they kept repeating a word like it should have a whole lot of meaning to me. "What's a gazebo?"

All three look confused, but only for a second. "Azibo," one enunciates—the one that was with Preta—and the mossy things above his eyes slash down just like eyebrows and he looks like he's worried I'm super stupid. Something seems to dawn on him, some comprehension. "You *really* can't care for her alone."

Exactly my fears, as well as my reality, and fuck him very much for pointing that out. "And you just happen to want the job, that it?"

Now his strips of moss scrunch together and he turns to the other two for translation, and it's my turn to look confused. "How is it you two can follow me but this clown can't?"

"*Clown,*" the dumbnut mouths, and he doesn't have to understand a damn word I say to get that I'm insulting him.

I realize with a hard nip of fear that antagonizing the alien life forms that have full access to Preta is a supremely stupid, *stupid* thing to do.

"You blooded our heartstones," the big one pipes up, tapping his chest.

Yeah. *That* was fuckin' weird too: they tried to get me to kiss rocks, and I've seen enough prison riots to know shit coming at your mouth is only the beginning, and when they steadied my head for it, I thought they're going to break my teeth, and I was about to have a mouthful of alien dic—

But they just tapped rocks against my lips and then popped them into holes in their chests. Plants started moving on top of them, big pink flowers sprouted, but at that point I figured the combo of help-lessness, panic, and fury was making my eyes see things. Now though, I'm staring at their very serious faces and it's hitting me that they're aliens—why is it so hard to believe their hearts are rocks and they can do things with plants that would make the Gardener's Association back home bust a nut?

Wait—I kissed their rocks, and they can understand me?

I look at Preta's rapist.

Not fucking happening.

"Settle yourself, neron," the big one says with a sigh. Translation: *simmer down, man.* "There is no need to feel territorial against *us.* We will protect her with our lives, just as you do."

I'm waiting for the taunting edge to his words, but it doesn't happen. He just keeps talking like this is all a given.

"Having more to feed and care for her can only be good, yes? You will need our help until you heal."

Not trusting, but feeling like I'm landing somewhere between there and hope, I finally manage, "All right. What's an 'azibo?'"

Nice Hands is all patience, like he's aware I'd totally know what it is and he's only supplying the explanation for this foreign word so that I'm on the same page. "An azibo is—" he starts, but my translator's caught up to it now, and I snarl as my body jolts, causing my leg to get jacked up.

"—a mate. We will be woven to her, and through the Sproutling... we are all connected," he finishes, looking at me in dismay now. Like, 'great, we're stuck with this crazy bastard,' because, 'simmer down, neron' or not, if I'm understanding the impression I'm getting both from my words and inside my head correctly, they intend to *share* Preta. With me.

Oh, *hell* no.

My brain fires away at this, and I point to Preta's rapist. "Did you make her kiss your—" I grit my teeth, count a breath, and spit, "rock?" I slam two fingers over my chest where my aliens' rocks went, and I see he's got a rock too, with little... orange... flowers... I cut a glance at Preta's hair and a red haze covers my vision.

"My heartstone?" He looks to the other two, then back to me, and nods.

I turn on the other two. You think I'm your—" I don't pause my words, but I feel my ballsack shrivel, "'azibo?'"

They look fuck-all confused. "She's our azibo. You're our tribesman, fellow husbandman."

"You two," I point to them, "don't fucking touch her, got me?" I am in no place to make demands, but it'd be awesome if they didn't know it, and I'm not sure what I'm dealing with intelligence-level wise, so why not try for the big dawg position?

...Doesn't work.

Nice Hands looks unimpressed. "You would refuse her feeding? Starve her?" Now he's starting to look disgusted—at *me*, like I'm worse than three aliens wanting to have their turn on her—so I clarify.

"No. You can fucking bring her food whenever she wants food. But you don't touch her."

I've got three confused aliens staring at me. I run my tongue over my teeth and lean my shoulder against the hard-packed wall behind me. "What part didn't you understand?"

"You can't be this dense," the tall one says easily—not smirking, but it's not a friendly smile either. "We will have her also, and you will accept it. This will keep her nourished and provide for her better. Set aside your pride and see that you have not been able to care for her properly—"

CHAPTER 15

MACEOUS

WHEN WE CLOSE THE DOOR on his ridiculous efforts—ridiculous because there is no way he has the power to make himself so much as rise and walk, which only serves to infuriate him further—I release a sigh that is nowhere in the vicinity of relief. "We can be pleased that he cares enough not to wake her if he can help it," I say at last.

Not taking his eyes from the door, Petrichor intones, "That one is damaged."

Knowing that our new tribesman won't be likely to calm at the reminder, something we're attempting to give him time to obtain, my voice is pitched low when I reply, "Considering what we came upon, I'd say he has every reason to be this protective of her."

Bortammos nods gravely. "Truth. Perhaps the attacking tribe has killed our azibo's other husbandmen. They looked ragged, and driven. Remember that there are tales of tribes that stalk and hunt each other, and in light of this possibility, his wild fury makes perfect sense."

Chor looks ready to collapse, *bole*-weary. "The matter of how to ease his concern is the question."

"Words do nothing," I remind them. "Actions prove everything. We have to show our new tribesman that we'll be good husbandmen. We can start by healing his leg."

Ammos looks at the supplies in the basket, what's left of them. "I have a few things I want to make first, then we should go gathering. He'll need that poultice changed frequently."

CHAPTER 16

PRETA

WHEN I OPEN MY EYES and see Ryan, words are leaving my mouth before my brain has a chance to catch up. "Y'werShot!" I croak, my lips not entirely awake yet, but he covers my mouth with his hand—softly, just a warning to be quiet.

"I'm fine. It's not serious, but I'm not walking out of here any time soon."

"What did it hit? Through and through, or...?"

"Took a chunk of my thigh muscle. We'll call it a deep graze." He snorts at himself. "Look," he locks his gaze on me, and I go tense. "Forget that for now. What do you remember before you woke up just now?"

"We..." my memories are weird. Dream creatures, and... I look at my hand. I look *under* my hand—we're lying on a giant pile of leaves. Not dry and crunchy, or wet just... green, suede-textured long leaves. I've got what looks like a freaky spider pelt on top of me. I look up at Ryan, who is wearing clothes while I am *not*, what the... "How did we get here? Where are we? Why did we have sex in an alien cave?"

And I see it.

He's wearing this grim, pained smile and it scares the crap out of me. At the finish of my last question, it's barely imperceptible, but his eyebrows twitch towards each other, and two tiny creases at the edges of his eyes appear for the briefest second.

And I know that the next words out of his mouth are going to be a lie.

"Don't," I tell him. The good news is that I don't think he's lied to me before, now that I'm seeing this.

His mouth hangs open for a beat before his head tips up, in sort of a nod—except that it doesn't come back down. "Micro Expressions, right. I pulled a double shift that day so that I could be there when they took you to the lab, and so that I could be the one to escort you back."

"I remember that day," I say softly, recalling it with the fuzzy, half-lucidity of the drugged. "That was the first time you touched me."

His eyes go comically round. "That sounds bad. It was a *hug*."

Without warning, I feel a smile beaming across my face. "Uh huh."

He levels me with a glare that lights up my insides, and makes my smile turn into a slightly evil grin, I'm pretty sure.

But all my humor dies when his expression leaches to one of sadness. Regret. Guilt.

Despite him being the guard, and me being the prisoner he towed around, Ryan never took advantage of me. He never touched me in a sexually inappropriate manner and *I* was the one who propositioned *him*. Not because it would get me favors, or protection, or anything useful; I was attracted to him, and I let him know. He responded, and we enjoyed mutual satisfaction, simple as that. None of our encounters were forced, or coerced, and I know that—but somebody here *did* take advantage of me. An *alien*. "They raped me?"

My voice is so calm that I'm startled. *I'm* so calm that I'm startled.

Ryan looks like he's about to pick up a twenty-foot caber and throw it—if his leg wasn't messed up and if we had twenty-feet of caber for him to vent on. He looks furious. He looks sick. He looks sorry.

He moves to draw me into a hug. "Preta..."

I don't push him away, but I redirect by grabbing his fingers and holding them. "I'm fine."

And... I am. I don't hurt anywhere. I don't really remember it, and what I think I remember, I thought it was Ryan. Unless something crops up later, sharper memories or some such, I'm going to be able to pick up and move on without becoming emotionally crippled. "How do we get out of here? I need clothes."

His arm is still suspended towards me, connected to me by my fingers. With his other hand, he points in my face. "Fuckin' weird, how you can do that."

I pull my head back so that he's not bopping me in the nose. "What's weird?"

"You turn it off. It's like your emotions are there. Then they aren't. They gave you a coping mechanism."

He sounds both horrified and awed.

I might be feeling both too, but he's right; it feels like my concern is turned off. I'm not awed so much as I'm grateful not to have to deal with my own emotional fallout. I wonder if I can control this on/off switch I've been provided. I snort. Provided. Like their intention was a gift.

My snort makes Ryan twitch, and he's going to rub that buzzed layer of nubby fluff right off his head if he keeps dragging his hand over it like that.

He eyes me. "You don't want to... talk about it?"

He looks mixed parts concerned, relieved, and angry.

I eye him back. "Do *you* need to talk about it?"

His hand leaves his hair and makes a fist to match his other. Oh no; he doesn't need to *talk* about this—he needs to beat the *shit* out of something. I look at his bandaged leg. He's kind of S.O.L. "How bad is your pain level?"

He glares down at his leg. "It should feel worse than this. They forced some sticky shit down my throat. It hurts, but I'm sitting up and not screaming, so..." he shrugs—but instead of loose, relaxed hands, they're still balled up, the veins standing out starkly. He actually looks really hot, and I've always had a thing for arm porn, but when I move to stand, he glances at the leaf-bed, to the massive wet spot that pooled under me.

Awkward. *Well, this'll help him calm down, yeah.*

"So," I attempt to move past the moment, "what do we do?"

Honestly, my dad was great, but reading fables wasn't his style. He told stories, and sure, read the two fox, one box, black socks rhyming-type books, but fables, not so much, and therefore, I'm not clear on how it goes exactly, but there's this one about a lion, a thorn, and a mouse, and if the lion turned and snapped at the mouse for touching the thorn—then I definitely should have taken the initiative to read up on this tale. Maybe if I'd learned the lesson from a book, I wouldn't have this snarling lion in my face as my reality right now.

"I can't DO ANYTHING! I CAN'T EVEN PROTECT—" he cuts himself off, biting down on his knuckles as if sinking his teeth into his own skin will keep them out of mine. But the blue line throbbing alongside his temple tells me that injury, plus helplessness, plus worry does not a settled man make.

Meanwhile, my soldier senses say my teammate is as safe as we can reasonably consider one to be in this situation, and... someone should do reconnaissance.

Ryan is not going to like this plan.

I can't actually tell if they downloaded successful missions from the past directly into my brain, but if it were me on this bed, and Charlie was the one up-and-able, I know what she'd do.

If it were Charlie on this bed, and it was our dad who was the one up-and-able, I know what *he'd* do.

...Yet I know if it were one of them on this bed, and *I* announced my intention, I'm pretty sure Charlie and my dad would say this is a *'too stupid to live'* plan.

I roll my eyes. *Baby-of-the-family syndrome.*

I wrap my hairy blanket tighter around me and start to search—and thankfully, I find my jumpsuit. It's folded and under a strongly scented, slightly warm bag of what could be alien potpourri.

"What are you doing?" His expression turns *gutted.* *"No.* Preta, you can't go out there!"

I toss the blanket onto the bed and shake out the *saffron* monstrosity. *Charlie, please be okay.*

Inside my head, I scoff loudly. *It's* Charlie. *She's fine.*

My nudity stuns him silent, I think. Me too, actually—I don't see my ribs punching against my skin, and... I don't feel as if I'm *starving.* I ponder this as I jam myself into my eyesore of an ensemble... if a one-piece qualifies as an ensemble. Surprisingly, my sexy suit isn't any worse off than it was earlier when I was walking around sweating in it, and actually, it smells better. Must be the potpourri. I flip it over in my hands, studying it until I see it has a little *face,* and it's peering right back at me. Large orb eyes, a bulbous nose, and long, magenta, ruffle-edged ears are what I initially mistook for dried petals; it smells good. And what I mistook for satchel mesh is its weird little skin.

Carefully, I set it on a primitive looking end table next to the water pitcher, and I see that Ryan has a potpourri pet on his side too. Decorating with live pets certainly makes the accommodations interesting. Like hotels giving guests pet goldfish. Question is, why are the aliens providing amenities for us captives? I mean that's what we are, right? This all feels very familiar: grabbed, crammed in holding room, violated without consent. Does a shower come with the Platinum Captive package? I hope someone ticked that box for me because I want to be signed up for this subscription. Also, underwear and a bra would be nice, and I didn't miss the fact that mine have disappeared.

"Preta."

His eyes are pleading with me, begging me not to go out alone.

Old Preta, the powered-by-Folgers Preta, would stay.

I feel the other presence in my head though. The one that wants to me to do what I have to do to protect my team—*him.* I may be pregnant, but I am currently the only member with mobility at the moment. "I have to know what's beyond that door." As far as we're aware, staying in here is no safer than stepping out of this room—but I'm not going to point this out to him because it's obvious he's infuriated enough with his bum leg as it is. It's stupid to make promises we both know I can't keep—but I can promise him this much: "I'll play it careful."

He nearly falls off the bed making a lunge for me.

I feel horrible, but inside, I'm being *driven* to see what we're up against.

His snarling gets louder when I open the round-topped, thick-planked door, and for how big this door is, I'm surprised when I can still hear his cursing perfectly well after I close it behind me. Mmm. Soundproofing: nil.

I fully expected to step out and see monsters. What I don't expect are three rather concerned human...ish... faces staring back at me.

All of them are covered in vines and flowers.

I shake myself. They were *dragons* just before everything got really crazy—vines and flowers, I can handle. I peer at them, aware I'm staring, but unable to stop. Thankfully, they stand very still, and I appreciate that they don't seem to mind my curiosity at all. None of them are acting aggressive, or threatening, which is what I stepped out expecting, so I'm feeling more than a little thrown.

When three sets of eyes shift to something on the side of my head, I realize I'm fiddling with the thing I feel there. Slowly, I pull it out, having a very good idea of what it is.

A little fire-orange flower.

I raise my eyes slowly, and lock on the brilliantly colored fire-flowers all across the middle one's body.

"Are you well?" one of them asks.

Whoa, whoa—wait. They can speak Human?

What does this mean? Does he have a translator too, and it pings off a signal in ours and uploads everything, or have they captured humans before somehow, and there happened to be an English speaker among the poor schmucks?

And 'am I *well?*' As if he genuinely cares to know.

I tap my flower back in place. I wasn't sure how I was going to play this, but here I stand playing nothing, because this is yet another game board I don't recognize.

How frustrating.

"Azibo?"

My translator must have been pulling overtime while I was out, because it supplies, *'mate.'*

One of them breaks away to approach me, and offers me a pile of leather-like material. Lifting the top item, I see it's more than a bikini top and less than a vest, and this bottom half here is basically a mini skirt made out of a purple spotted giraffe, if giraffes had skin textured with elephantine wrinkles. And... lichen? The lichen seems to be growing happily out of the hide.

Okay. I accept them graciously even though it's going to take me a minute to build up the willpower to walk back in to a frightened, bitey Ryan vying for me to stay with him while I undergo my costume change. I could change out here; prison has a way of breaking you from being shy, but prison also has a way of teaching you that some men see invitations in all sorts of circumstances. Apparently one of them already had a good time; I'd just as soon not tempt the others.

"Are you hungry again?"

Still surprised that I can understand him, I pause too long and he gestures to my stomach. "I fed you. You were in great need. I believe you will need to eat often."

"Fed me, huh?" Drogan didn't mention unconscious feeding, then again, he was worried about my emotional damage. All in all, I'd rank being fed pretty far down on the 'it was terrible, are you okay' list of discussion topics too. In this case, without gnawing aches, without morning sickness or lab drug sickness, and with no obvious soreness or even bruises that I saw of from them enjoying themselves while I was out of it—I'm feeling better than normal.

"Yes. Your seedling must take much from you."

"My..." I know all about government contracts; they take the lowest bids almost all of the time, and sometimes, that gets shoddy results. Workmanship just isn't what it used to be.

My translator is obviously one of these casualties.

Thanks, Concord Prison Ship: you will not be getting a five-star rating from me.

"You seem restless." He examines me quickly without heat. "Restless, but rested. Restored." His eyes flick to the door at my back and I tense.

He doesn't miss it.

Way to play your hand, Sol.

He's eyeing me carefully as he says, "We were about to refill our supplies for poultices. Would you like to go along?"

"You'll let me outside." My tone may or may not convey a heavy dose of disbelief.

He looks unsure. "Let?"

I don't want to give him ideas but he can't be stupid.

"After what happened in there—" I cut myself off because he doesn't leer, he doesn't get angry that I'm pointing it out, he doesn't grab me and throw me down and relive another conquest. He actually looks... confused.

"Ceremony?"

Now it's my turn to wear his look. "Ceremony," I repeat slowwwly.

"Ceremony," he confirms, this time with pride, but not in a creepy way. Oddly, he manages it in a completely non-threatening vibe entirely.

He appears to be having difficulty grasping where the problem is with this plan, and I'm not going to enlighten him. Stupid captors make escape options more likely. Though, he doesn't appear stupid; he's got sharp eyes—striking eyes, actually, spotted with yellows and greens like a Cattleya-orchid.

If they're going to attack me, they're going to attack me. Location isn't going to change that, however, learning the lay of our land isn't a bad idea—not that we'll be able to move any time soon. A leg wound takes weeks to heal from—and that's IF it doesn't get infected.

"Let me tell Ryan," I test, but the alien only nods and looks perfectly accommodating. I know this is going to upset him, so I don't walk into the bedroom; I just pop open the door and lean my head in to mouth "I'm going to be fine. I'll be back: don't freak out."

It's a good thing I didn't waste my breath actually speaking out loud, because Ryan completely ignores my *I'm going to be fine* and *don't freak out* and must read something along the lines 'I'M GOING TO TAKE A WALK WITH MY RAPIST.'

He struggles like his leg is not going to stop him from reaching me this time—he's wicked-freaked. I see this, but I can either hide in bed and wait for the shoes to drop, or I can try to do some recon. Sending him as reassuring of a look as I can manage, I pull back.

"Preta, *NO!*"

Quietly, I close the door between us. When I turn, it isn't victorious smirks I see on the three aliens waiting for me. Instead, as my eyes target each of their faces, and I take in their postures, expressions; it's discomfort that I read, unease—especially on two of them.

"Lead the way," I say politely, and watch in no little amazement when they courteously nod and do just that.

CHAPTER 17

"HOW FAR ALONG IS YOUR Sproutling?"

This comes from the one who had sex with me—Petrichor, he politely informed me when he insisted we exchange names, breaking all the rules about not humanizing victims—as we help each other over yet another log. He doesn't walk well, which I guess shouldn't be strange since he probably spends a lot of time as a tree-dragon. It's just that he didn't have this problem when he carried *me,* and the other one seems fine. Then again, maybe the other one has more practice at walking on two legs; what do I know?

I shrug. This bumps Petrichor's arm, which is slung over my neck. That had been something else; we'd been marching along, and on maybe the third time he'd nearly gone down, I slipped under his arm, like it was the most natural thing in the universe to help an alien out. Although, *we've already had sex,* so maybe this is my programming glomming on and being super helpful. Which is ridiculous. I should be karate-chopping him, not propping him up. Fricking Mary Sue programming. "My... sproutling?" These prison-issue shoes are crap. They weren't designed for comfort and they certainly weren't designed for durability on an alien planet and because I'm not wearing any socks, my heels have been rubbed raw and they're *killing* me.

I look up when Petrichor doesn't say anything further, and when he sees that he has my attention, he gestures to my stomach.

Said stomach clenches. And *this* is my limit. I've rolled with everything, not so much as a twitch until *the baby.* The baby is my soft-spot.

Everything suddenly feels ice-cold. I don't know; maybe I'm super suspicious, but having your alien defiler armed with the knowledge of your early stage pregnancy when you've neither told him nor are you showing enough for him to guess is somehow unsettling and seems like a bad, bad portent.

I'm not sure what he reads off of my face, but the look he shoots me is a deeply offended one. "I'm not a threat, Preta."

At a tap on my shoulder, I take a break from playing teammate with Petrichor, slipping out from under his arm and turning. The alien that came along with us (the tallest one stayed with Ryan) presses a triangular, heavy, watermelon-pink goodie at me. I know it's a goodie, because he's got the other half of it in his mouth. He swallows before saying, "For the Sproutling. He craves sweets."

No way... I actually have been jonesing for something with sugar. "Thank you, Bortammos... can I just call you Bort? Or Ammos? Is that okay? My... uh, my people—my kind?—like nicknames, if that's all right."

He ducks his head. "Of course. I'd be honored."

My translator got all of his words this time. I'm impressed at how fast it's zipping along, considering it was only intended to learn human languages. I look to the other alien. "And can I call you...?"

"Chor. Please call me Chor." Petrichor looks very pleased.

With a nod to both of them, I take a tentative nibble off of the pink food, and despite the crumbly texture, it hits the sugar-gimmies so good that I sigh in utter bliss.

"Very good," Ammos murmurs, and he's smiling at my stomach, like he senses approval from the tiny baby inside me that is very happy right now.

He can tell what the baby is craving—this is crazy!

"I don't know when I will be able to feed you again," Chor informs me as I take my next bite. "This is why Bortammos has come along. You will need to tell him when you get hungry."

I glance back and wiggle my fruit, "Thank you, I'm good."

When I face forward though, Petrichor has moved so close that I almost collide with him. I have to crane my neck in order to see his face now, and he's smiling like he thinks I'm the cutest thing. *Bad, bad portent.* Stupidly though, my insides warm a little. I guess everyone likes being liked?

"The other hunger," he says with a quiet laugh.

Blinking, I trail after him, and when I finish my sweet, Bortammos offers me a damp leaf. The jungle version of a wet napkin, aha.

I keep a special eye on Petrichor, and part of me is watching for him to do something cruel or threatening. If I hadn't woken up to the mess between my legs, I'd never have believed he'd done anything to make me a victim. I wasn't sore, I felt better than I had in a long time, actually, and he didn't harm me in any way besides, well, have sex with me when I *wasn't lucid.* I thought I was having a really great dream with Ryan, not having very real sex with an alien. As far as I can see it, there are two possibilities: Petrichor is a sociopath, or he doesn't feel that having sex with me without my express permission is wrong.

Neither of these are great options, but the second one might be more workable. At least less... dangerous. If he's a decent guy... erm, *alien*—he could be informed, and reasoned with. Slim chances, but if I get a choice, I'll take 'was ignorant' over 'he disregards my basic human rights.'

Ahhh, *human* rights. Being that he's never seen one before—at least I don't think—he thinks I'm *his* kind of female and so I'm getting the impression this is all well and good if you are a lady tree-dragon. I have explained I am not, but for someone who lives inside of a tree in a hole in the ground, it just means I'm from another tribe. I will give him this; he's taken every one of my answers in stride. Me coming from far, far away doesn't faze him. He has no concept of planets and Earth, and no matter how I try to explain, to him it just sounds like a couple days' walk from here. Crash landing? He's just *'glad you are all safe,'* referring to me, the Sproutling, and Ryan. There's a third option, but it's an offshoot of the first. He thinks I'm his mate, that because he made me come, he did all the right things, like hitting all the buttons for the winning sequence with the old Simon Says game, so to him... nothing about what he did with me was wrong. Again with my hope that he can be reasoned with...

I flick a glance back at Ammos, and catch him staring at me, and like all of the other times we've already done this, he looks away quickly. He seems shy.

Whenever I do this, casting my gaze towards Ammos, Petrichor will let our conversation lull like he's giving me time to peruse his friend, like he knows I'm as curious about them as they are about me.

Petrichor has mostly rounded ears like a human, but Bortammos' are *alien*. A little tapered, a lot of greenery—not his color, because he's brown, but actual tiny growing plantlife on the tips—but both of them can move their ears. They are forward whenever I talk, but when I send a direct stare his way, Ammos' drop flat. It looks more submissive than aggressive.

Not that I'm trying to stir him up; I'm just curious.

So are they. As we go along, me stuffing what they hand me into a pouch at my waist, they are asking loads of questions. "Past the great waters?"

I hesitate, trying to think of how best to explain this. I've been trying to describe where Earth is and I'm having absolutely no success. "There are great waters but it's off the planet, like the stars, but way beyond them and..." I trail off, seeing no recognition on their patiently watching faces. It's a concept they just can't fathom.

"We have never flown past the great waters. Dangerous territory," Chor comments, and he looks at me with a heaping amount of—unwarranted—respect for not only me being assumedly brave, but successful.

"Our great waters are different than your great waters," I finish with a little grimace.

He pets my shoulder though, and it makes my insides happy.

A little *too* happy.

As Chor continues to be everything curious about my 'tribe'—and Ammos starts to jump in more and more frequently with quiet inquiries, I try to determine why it's making me feel so... content. Ryan's laid up, hurt, alone with an alien and worrying himself sick, I have no doubt—and I'm worried about *him*, yet I'm feeling... peaceful. I wanted to know what we were up against, and I got that. And I'm feeling more settled than I have since before my sentencing to the *Concord*.

We're hunting for leaves—*LEAVES*—but it doesn't matter. It makes my brain happy. The group activity is invigorating.

Hive mentality. This walk is satisfying a desire I should probably be disturbed over, but getting freaked would be pointless; I can't change what was done to me, and knowing why I'm feeling this way helps me set it all aside—*it's programming*—I can struggle against it, or I can accept it.

Specifically, our group activity is collecting zemerac leaves. Well, the guys are collecting zemerac leaves. I'm not tall enough to reach the ones with the red-undersides, so I'm basically here to cheer them on, and they are helping my recon plan, because they are showing me trails and they *want* me to get familiar with this place; I don't have to cleverly pry loose the information because their answers and their questions don't stop. Which is good, because my translator is soaking this up: what tribe am I from? Did I choose Ryan, or did he trade for me? How many husbandmen did I have...?

Well, the translator tries. I smack the back of my head twice, wishing there was a way to calibrate this thing.

Seeing me hit myself disturbs the other two though, so I send them an 'it's all good' smile and go back to doing the rah-rah as they inspect zemerac and stuff them into pouches tied near their skimpy green loincloths.

Did you know that jungle aliens basically show off all the goods when they stretch up high? They are fantastically muscled and when they aren't being tree-dragons, they have the kind of bodies human men would kill to own.

I smirk to myself. *Human women would kill to own these bodies too.*

I'm not leering at them or anything; I'm curious. I'm basically a researcher right now. *A researcher who is contemplating how a woman would climb them.* When one holds out a new variety of leaf for my inspection, trying to explain what it does when it's steeped in hot water, I'm hearing his every word, but not eyeing the offering he intends. I'm watching his arm muscles flex.

My thighs clench, and without panties, I feel my wetness run down the inside of my leg.

Oh no. This right here was what I was afraid of back on the *Concord.* I've only felt a low-level desire all day, and that's abnormal, because I usually have to corner Ryan twice a shift, but when it really hits, I'm ready to jump anybody and I was always relieved that I had Ryan, who would double back to the cells on his off-hours to take care of 'paperwork,' or whatever he had to claim in order to get me out and give us a chance to be alone, however temporary. It wasn't easy; the responsibility had to fall to him to manipulate the roster, the timeclock, the shift changes, the inmate transfers, and camera coverage—he made sure we were taken care of so that I could get this out of my system safely.

When I return my attention to the guys, it's to see them both staring at me, and I don't have to ask: they must be able to smell or sense my situation somehow, judging by the looks on their faces. "I need Ryan," I inform them. "I need Ryan *right now.*"

"You *are* hungry," Petrichor states.

I'm not even capable of answering him—I'm pretty sure my mouth is hanging open. The other hunger. *The other hunger.* That's what he'd said to me earlier. How would they know I'd get hungry for sex? How *could* they know this?

They sense things, they have to: first the pregnancy, now this.

...And back up, Bortammos came along for the ride—like, *for the ride,* for the ride!

I swing a very wide-eyed stare to him.

Tiny vines trail over his cheekbones like a blush and he averts his face quickly. Ears dropping flat, his hand scratches across his chest in what I believe is a nervous move, but it only draws my attention to the carved muscle of his incredibly fit, uncannily human-like torso.

In overall form. Obviously not in texture.

Somehow, it's still ridiculously hot.

I cover my eyes.

I haven't seen a naked man in months, not since before I got to the *Concord.* Whenever, um, *sexual congress* occurred with my *guard,* I was the only one that had to half-disrobe in order to make sex happen. It was a quick affair in all the ways, so this visual buffet—*despite growing flora*—here should be an opportunity to satiate an itch that's been growing for a while... except that I'm *not* feeling satiated. And this 'hunger' is getting worse.

"I *need* Ryan." *What will they do?*

I peek when I sense Bortammos stepping away, taking his tempting muscles with him, looking resigned, and Petrichor is watching me like he can read my mind and that's as equally unsettling, but whether he can or can't, at least he doesn't push. "Have another fruit for now," is all he says before he turns and starts to snatch the tree bald of the red leaves. He's moving fast, reaching up high—

He staggers, poultice-making-supplies going in every direction as he crashes to the ground.

CHAPTER 18

RYAN

I DON'T KNOW HOW LONG we do the silent stare down. By the time my eyes are burning bad enough that I have to blink, and after I've played the mental gymnastics it takes to decide this isn't a concession—I can blink without losing, dammit—I stay locked on him for what feels like another forever as the asshole across from me just stares right fucking back.

It goes on for so long like this, I want to haul off and cave his teeth in. Maybe he doesn't realize how confrontational this is. He *is* a motherfucking alien. Nostrils flaring, I spit, "There a reason we're doing this?"

The alien smiles. "Good. You gave in first."

I lunge for him.

He catches me like a person grabs a little kid; big-ass hand is planted under my chest, shoving me upright, then slamming down on my shoulder to keep me from trying it twice. "I'm beginning to suspect that you have the intelligence of a ground mushroom, with only enough extra mobility to be a nuisance."

"I'll KILL Y—"

His other hand pops over my mouth, and he shakes his head, and I did not know just how threatening this move was until just now. My hands are wrapped around his wrist, but I'm not fucking *strong* enough to budge him. What's got me tweaking the most is this tiny kernel of what feels a lot like fear.

"I am going to take my hand away. Ask what you really want to ask."

Is this a game? I'm afraid to show where my weak spot is, but it isn't like he doesn't know. He has to know. "What are you doing to Preta?"

He nods, and finally, his gaze dips, and I feel myself relax a centimeter. "She is well. Here, let me change your poultice while we speak." He motions to where they cut flaps in my pant leg in order to clean and pack the bullet graze. "Bortammos and Petrichor are taking the chance to get to know her, and giving her the same opportunity. This is good. You have to see... we are not like the males you knew."

Asshole, you have no idea.

The alien stares at me some more. To say I don't fucking appreciate it would be an understatement.

I crack my knuckles and take a much-needed second to think. My leg pain is going killer on me right now, which is not making it any easier to concentrate. And *that* makes me think, because it's not like the movies where a gunshot wound means the hero runs around and does all the things. In real life, if you take a bullet, you are not doing all the things. It pretty much means you're not doing any of the things.

As I lie here, fighting infection and having dead *plants* changed out, I know my odds are bad. If I die, Preta's alone. If we hadn't been... *saved* by the jolly green giants, the best scenario out of what went down back there would be her miraculously escaping and probably starving to death before infection even got a chance to take me out.

Whatever the Clown did to her... it helped her. He made her healthy. If I die, she's stuck alone with aliens, but they could have really hurt her, and they didn't, and they don't have to take the time to explain a damn thing, but they are, and there's a lot of things they could have done to make the situation worse since we came, but they haven't.

I'm struggling, but I can say it: it could be worse.

This... this isn't all a bad thing. Not necessarily.

The colony quirk she has is going to love this setup, and sure, it's not what the research team intended, but she's essentially a lab experiment that made it to the wild. It's like the dinosaur-island movie said: shit's bound to adapt and find a way.

The tall one finishes changing the pesto-paste crap on my wound, nodding to himself with whatever he's seeing. "You know of tribes that will kill off competing males."

Not a question, but also not a threat, despite how threatening his words should feel.

I guess it's a true statement, as far as he'd understand from what happened in the clearing between the survivors from the Alpha pod anyway. "Yeah."

"We don't. The Kahav don't."

"The Kahav," I say slowly, and he seems pleased.

"You have heard of us before?"

I smile a little. "No, man. Can't say that I have."

"We operated as a good tribe, a healthy tribe, back when we had our own people."

As he tells me their fucking sad, and frankly terrifying history, I replay and review the valos' behavior.

That's what this planet is filled with. Valo. It's their version of human. The valos we were carried off by are the Kahav tribe.

What's left of them.

With only three males, they're feeling pretty damn lucky that Preta dropped into their lap. They think she's the answer to their lonely prayers.

I couldn't care less about them. But Preta...

She's *needed* a group. She's like the ants in the ant farm at the lab; she's driven to form a healthy hive that will work together, tackle assignments, and be useful as a team.

What the aliens have her out there doing right now. This is what she's been altered to do, kind of. I'm not so blind by fear, and concern, and yeah, jealousy, that I can't recognize that she's needed what they can offer her: a hive.

I'm not giving her up though.

Preta's mine.

So is the little Drogan-Sol.

I don't fucking share.

A fist is squeezing the shit out of my heart right now, and I drag the heel of my hand over my chest.

She needs them.

I look down at my leg.

I...

I can...

I. Can. Share.

For however long I've got left.

CHAPTER 19

BORTAMMOS

HAULING CHOR UP, I feel Preta brush against me as she takes one of Chor's arms across her shoulders in an effort to assist. "That log over there," I direct her, and she helps me deposit his bulk where he won't fall far if he loses the struggle for balance again. I could have easily managed his transplantation myself, but I like that she was near me and *not* testing me. All this stretch, I've felt her measuring me, and for a withering moment, when she asked for Ryan to be the one to feed her, I had to believe she found me lacking.

Oversensitive in regards to myself, but not sensitive enough *to her*—of course she'd be more comfortable with the husbandman she's had the longest. I shake my head as I check with Chor. "You seem drained in the extreme."

He looks at Preta, who appears sweetly concerned. He gives me a fatigued smile. "It was worth it."

I make quick work of recollecting everything that he dropped, and I bring it to Preta. "Here. I will take you both back."

I hand her my leather pack too, because unlike the loincloth which is made from plant fiber, the pack won't change with me when I shift. Her eyes are a little wide when I approach her in my Guardian form, but she tries to help me get Chor into my hands before she joins him.

I'm hyperaware of her increasing hunger.

So is she.

My cupped palms ensure that neither one of them will tumble out of my hands during the flight back, but it also means that they are pressed up against one another, and its accelerating her need.

110

By the time we arrive back at the warren, I can tell that we're all bracing for her husbandman's reaction. I'm surprised, *relieved beyond measure,* when his gaze is steady and there is acceptance in his eyes. He isn't thrilled, that's clear enough, but he isn't going to attack her despite them having different ways than our own tribe. He must genuinely care about her, and what *she* requires.

Concurrently, she *is* hungry, but this is what she wanted: to return to him. A flower can't be taken from the shade and abruptly thrust into full sunlight nor vice-versa—it is gradual process wherein a delicate hand reaps the sweetest bounty.

Yet, I consider his injured leg and doubt that, even if he possesses nectar to feed her, that he will be able to take root inside of her. They must be aware of this also, as she is taking utmost care as she moves to sit next to him. She can't wait long, but it is only natural that her husbandman get a private moment with her, to ascertain her treatment and feelings in this matter if nothing else.

I try to call her name, but my mouth is too dry, as if the apprehension caused the stomates on my tongue to release all the moisture. After a pause that goes on too long to be comfortable for either of us—*any* of us since everyone's eyes are on us now—I manage, "Are you... desperate?"

"*No,*" she answers quickly.

We both wince. That was too quick to be quite believable. I can, of course, also hear the Sproutling clamoring, and she must remember this because her cheeks react with a rapid pigment shift and her hand moves towards her stomach before she drops it with a nervous clap against her leg.

Unsure what to say, I overgroom the flower budding on my wrist, and a petal tears.

I pull my fingers back sharply, too disturbed to heal it.

I *rival* her in the need for a reprieve, I realize.

They are on Chor's bed, so Mace moves to assist a still-weakened Petrichor, saying only, "Let's get him to my room. I'll ready-up one of the others for my own tonight."

They step out, heading down the tunnel, but I hesitate. When I chance a look at Preta's face, she is watching me go, holding one side of her bottom lip in her teeth—and as I struggle to meet her eyes, I see her lip slowly curve up.

My ears slap against the side of my head and I nearly flee the room.

Destination reached, I crowd in behind my tribesmen, and as Chor feebly situates himself on Mace's bed, Mace directs his words to me even though they are for both of us. "He's coming around, I think. Continue to be patient with him. It seems this is new to them both. Having more than one husbandman is not done in their tribe."

My eyes widen, thinking of her condition when she arrived. "It's a wonder their females have survived to carry on the next generation."

Mace nods, agreeable in this. "She looks as if she requires another feeding already. The Sproutling certainly says so," he says with a tilt of his lips. Then he adds, "I have a vejo-kaolin left."

My eyes travel to a cage in the corner, and I spy it watching us, its fluffy face appearing inquisitive and harmless. "You're offering to forfeit a full coat?"

Mace shrugs. "It would make a nice gift."

I regard him a moment. What it would *make* is a goodwill impression, and it is *Mace's* gift to give—he should be the one to cultivate this tie. "Are you certain?"

In response, Mace retrieves it, adding only, "Chor. Take it. He must be hungry by now. This is good." Then he grins. "Ask him if he requires help relieving himself yet."

I relish the last about as much as Ryan will, I'm sure. Cage clutched in my hands, this is how I find myself approaching him, as I wonder if this was such a good idea after all.

"What is that?" my new tribesman asks.

"It is a gift," I begin, but my voice falters when I flick a glance at Preta only to find that she is watching *me*. Although I have no trouble conversing with Ryan, I find I'm still unable to meet her eyes, but at least with a male presence, I'm comfortable enough I can speak mostly intelligently. "It is from Maceous." I feel he should know this, to know the importance of Mace's gesture. I want him to recognize the fact that we are attempting to make this situation an amiable one. "Have you had one before? They take a little getting used to, but they're very good."

"Can't say I have," is as much as Ryan allows.

Preta however, coos prettily over it, sounding delighted. "Can I pet it?"

"Uh, of course." I shake it from the cage, which is the same funnel-topped contraption it was captured in, and the moment its tiny toes hit my palm, it tries to bounce for my face. Anticipating this, I drop the cage and clap my hand over its head, and let it sink its teeth into my thumbs to give it something that will keep it still while she strokes the long fur along its back.

"It's so, so soft! It's like touching strands of powdered sugar! Oooh, Ryan, pet it."

Ryan's gaze is affixed to where the vejo-kaolin has ahold of me. "Nope. I'm good."

My heart sinks, hearing the dismissal in his voice.

From the corner of my eye, I see a strange change come over Preta. Her skin gets flushed, and her form stiffens, and I do not know what Ryan experiences, but I feel compelled to... to capitulate.

I blink, dazed.

Ryan stares at her a moment before he drops his gaze, eyes on his poultice as he exhales through his nostrils. "That was cool of Mace to share, but I'm getting that this isn't supposed to be a pet, is it?"

"No," I say at the same time Preta blurts, "What?"

She yanks her hand back when the vejo-kaolin releases me and whirls to bite her. I pinch the loose skin at its shoulders and place it back in the cage before examining the damage to my digits. Not too severe. It helps to know that in preparing for the treatment of Ryan's injury, we are well stocked in herbs so I'll be able to tend to it easily enough. I hand the cage to Ryan, who takes it with a wry smile. "It is food," I explain. "You pluck the fur like this," and I take hold of the hair that sticks through the bars, "and see how it tugs off easily? It doesn't hurt it. They need short summer coats or they overheat so capturing them is a kindness, though they don't always agree, as you can see."

"You eat their hair," is all Ryan says.

I hand him the piece I pulled off. "It is a delicacy. Nutrient-rich, but they are very hard to catch." I brace myself. "Mace asked me to check if you needed assistance relieving yourself yet?"

Ryan's expression goes dark. "Fucker." At another of Preta's looks—this one alarmed—he adds, "Him, not you. And it's fine, babe. The big motherfucker is just having fun with the crippled man."

When this doesn't calm her concern, he groans and scrubs a hand over his face. "You know what a nervous boner is?"

She nods uncertainly.

"Okay, know what happens when a guy needs to piss but gets a boner?"

Not directly watching her, I still see how her face colors.

"Yeah. He laughed his ass off. He's lucky my stream shut down, or he'd have been wearing it and *I'd* have been the one laughing. Fucker," he says again.

Unsure how to proceed from here, I carefully start, "...Well, I see he left you a bowl if you... need to," I finish, feeling desperately uncomfortable.

Ryan switches the subject. "Anything we can do about the lighting in here? You guys got candles or can you see in the dark?"

I try to answer him in the order he asked the questions. "You can turn on the lights if you like. We do have candles, and yes, we can see in the dark."

"Turn the lights on?" he asks without comprehension.

I point to the lever behind him.

Both he and Preta turn to examine it. Then he grabs the end and pulls it down.

The lights come on.

"*You have electricity?!*" Ryan shouts. "In a fucking hole in the ground!"

I look from one stunned face to the other and clarify, "Earth power?"

Ryan's face transforms from shock to confusion. "...Sure."

Preta moves to her hands and knees on the bed to crawl towards me, and the sight has my skin heating, and my ears wanting to lift with interest, all while my gaze suddenly feels weighted, pulling my scope of vision down to a spot at my feet.

She is not deterred by my inability to be at ease with her, thankfully. "Is there *running water?*"

"*Running...?*" I ask my toes.

"I need a bath." I hear a smile in her voice, and oddly, it doesn't settle my insides in the least.

"We can take you to the tarn tomorrow," I assure the floor.

"Tarn?"

At this, I do look up, but having her entire attention on me is too much to bear and I quickly find myself staring at my feet again. "A mountain pool. The water is warm."

"I'm in!" she declares.

"Are you hungry?" I squeeze my lids over my eyes, mortified at how awkwardly I managed to navigate the conversation to that question.

After the longest pause in Sonhadra's history in which I die a series of painful, humiliating deaths, she agrees. "I am."

CHAPTER 20

PRETA

I'M NOT THE ONLY ONE who can be *practical*—Ryan's dealing. He calmly fills me in on some things Chor and Ammos hadn't covered before Petrichor's fall happened.

Mates.

Alien mates.

Ryan's lips aren't hard against mine, but the kiss is fierce, and he's reluctant to let me go.

I can sympathize.

My stomach is not so good when I find myself following Ammos' stilted directions to his room. What's that old military term? BOHI-CA? *'Bend Over, Here It Comes Again.'* I take a deep breath, and enter it. Ammos is at the foot of the bed, staring at it like a man who has deep thoughts and many worries.

The sound of the door closing behind me makes him jump.

I have to force myself to blink. *He's even more nervous than I am.*

It has an oddly calming effect—on me, *definitely* not on him.

He suddenly can't stand still, and shies around to the other side of the bed, tucking in leaves here and there. When he sees he's got nothing left to neaten, he scans the rest of the room, ears pinning flat, and it's obvious he's desperately hoping something else will pop up. I duck a little and finally succeed at catching his eyes—only to watch him freeze. He twitches like he'd love nothing more than to break away, and look down.

This alien is painfully *shy.*

"Hey," I say softly, trying not to spook him. Or smile. I really want to smile but I really, really don't want to make him even more self-conscious than he already is. He is clearly not at a place where he can joke with me right now; this poor guy's nerves are way too high for anything that resembles teasing, I'm sure of it.

I want to ask why Mace didn't take on the part of 'feeding' me but to tell the truth, Mace sort of *intimidates* me—I don't *know* him—so... so I guess I can understand a little of what Ammos must be feeling right now.

I cut him a break and call a cease-fire to our eye contact as I cross the room and set my knee on the bed, more than half expecting him to run.

I think he more than half wants to.

I lie back, and instead of watching him, I try to keep my eyes on the ceiling, at the roots that hold everything together, that keep the dirt from crushing us alive. Slowly, walking resolutely, he makes his way to the end again and reluctantly climbs on, stopping before he gets to my toes.

I chance a glance at him and he drops his eyes, then flinches like he knew he shouldn't have. "S-sorry," he stumbles before he mutters under his breath, "She's going to starve to death at this pace."

I really, *really* want to smile. Not at his discomfort, but because I so sympathize with him over it. I sit up, and—not looking directly at him—ask; "Do you want to do this?"

His shoulders hunch and he drops a little lower, in a self-flagellating move, "Yes! I do, I badly do, I just... I'm not—"

He can't even finish his sentence, and his skin is getting browner in his cheeks and his ears and his moss-line.

I move to roll over, and as I do, I catch his look of concerned confusion, and plain regret, because he thinks he's blown this.

I'm now facing away from him, and it helps. This way, the pressure isn't on either of us. *This is still going to be weird...* I reach under myself, past my primitive little relative of the miniskirt, and begin stroking next to my clit.

"What—are... you...?"

His tone is so wonderstruck that I have to press my face into the leaves to prevent him from seeing what my lips are doing. When my throat stops jumping and I'm positive I won't laugh, I go for matter-of-fact when I answer, "I'm trying something less..."—*intimate*—"intense."

He utters a hoarse, "I don't think it's working."

I can't help it—the snort bursts out of me, and I flatten my front to the bed, shaking. I'm about to apologize when his large hand lightly grazes the outside of my thigh.

I nearly flinch out of surprise, but I catch the shift of my body in time to turn it into a hip sway.

Hesitantly, his hand repeats the stroke, but with more contact this time, less afraid he'll be rejected, or die, or whatever he's built up in his mind as the terrifying thing that will happen.

"You... want to... like this?" he sounds unsure in the extreme.

"Does this feel more comfortable? Not having to look me directly in the face?"

For a long moment I think maybe he's too shy/timid/reserved/choked/bashful to even answer, but he manages a deeply relieved-sounding, *"Yes. Thank you."*

Since he's not at the point where he's comfortable enough to touch me, I go back to playing with myself, and I take a thrill in hearing his breathing change—faster, louder, *hotter.*

Yes. Hotter can *be heard.*

When I'm self-lubed enough that the movements of my finger cause an audible slishing sound, he's overcome and groans, his hands cupping my hips before they take a slow slide to the curve of my butt, where he fills each hand with a cheek and squeezes.

I purr in satisfaction.

His hips press against my ass.

This surprises us both—but for my part, I may be startled, but the fact that he couldn't stop himself from doing it makes me even wetter.

Not wanting to lose progress, I let my hips sway and coax, "Do it again."

When he's ready, it's nothing at all for him to flip up my skirt. I'm not wearing my panties under this so he's got nothing holding him back.

Except nerves.

Are his hand shaking? He clears his throat. "Do you require prevernal pollen?"

That must be what I was hit with before. "Nope, I'm all good to go."

Am I curious? Yeah, I'm curious, but I'm pretty sure if I do look at what he's packing and I can't control my reaction to what I find, this alien will be done performing and perhaps scarred for life.

So I press my chest down harder against the leaves, and arch my back when I feel the tip of his—

My butt drops by instinct, my pelvis trying to flatten to the bed.

"Preta?" he asks, voice straining. "Is something wrong?" he has a pleasantly deep voice, and to hear the strain in it is weirdly exciting.

There's something alien about his dick. I pep talk myself—fast. *This was to be expected!* Pull it together, Preta!

"Preta?" and I feel his weight shift further away from me.

Great. Now I've freaked him out. This is so messed up. I'm giving an alien a penis complex and I have to soothe *him* when it's me that's got to take it—and considering that I've already had sex with Chor, apparently, I've already taken it.

It was good. That much I remember.

I force myself back to my hands and knees. "I'm ready."

Knees land on the outsides of mine. Tentative hands grab hold of my hips, and I feel a nudge against my pussy, yet it's *also* bumping my ass and my inner thigh.

At the same time.

This alien has what feels like multiple cocks.

I wonder if Chor did—*does*—too.

One of his hands leaves my hip, and he presses himself in, inhaling sharply before gently prodding in order to get deeper. Instead of thrusting like I expect though, I feel him... moving... inside of me.

I feel many *things* moving inside of me.

"Ammos?" I yelp—I can't help it, it's scaring me even though in my head I'm telling myself, *Shut up, Preta, it's fine!*

"Does it hurt?" he asks quickly, and I hear worry, and before I know it, he's sliding his hand from where it was gripping a handful of love handle, down to my belly and between my legs and—

I buck with an instant orgasm.

"Was that too much?" his hand leaves and he starts to pull back, which pulls his cock back, but... I can't help but notice that not *all* of him is retreating from me. It... seems like it has quite a reach.

It's fine, it's fine, stop freaking out, it's fine.

Eyes wide, I assure him, "It was good." I arch my back and wiggle a little, testing as I feel things fanning out inside of me. "Keep going."

Something tickles my g-spot.

I gasp, "Oh!"

"So wet," he says raggedly.

We are. The insides of my thighs feel cooler where air hits the wetness gathering there.

He may be the smaller of the three aliens, but he still dwarfs me by comparison, and I'm reminded of this when one of his big hands moves to my shoulder, cupping it and giving him the leverage he needs to go to poundtown.

Except he doesn't. His other hand plants next to my head, the veins standing in stark relief on his hand and along his forearm, *unnnf.*

"You're not taking nectar," he says hesitantly.

Nectar. I shake my head. "I don't know how."

My g-spot gets brushed again, making me jolt.

"Is that good?"

I feel them—*things*—gather and press at that inner marble of nerve-happiness. It feels like fingers. Long, flexible fingers. On his dick.

I'm not really in a position to complain, considering how good it's feeling.

"Here," he offers, and his hand comes over my mons again and I get another little taste of orgasm-magic.

"Good!" he chokes out, and I can feel what he means, because I'm coming, and he's filling me up with hot pulses that are making my insides happy.

So are his dick's funny fingers. They're vibrating. It shouldn't feel good, but it does. I'm squirming, impaled on the thicker base of him, feeling the longer fingers edging around my insides like they're alive and curious and I'm kind of creeped out, but having less and less of an issue with it as wave after wave of shudders roll through me. *Hell yeah, this is goooood!*

My ears are ringing. I think I screamed that.

His chest lands over my back and I bow under him, lifting myself higher, changing our angle, and now it's not just his dick's fingers dancing on my g-spot, his base is poking right on it.

Why isn't he moving?

I slam my butt against his muscled abdomen.

"Preta!" he gasps.

I roll my hips, and slam back again. "Fuck me!" I beg-and-order him.

"Do what?"

He sounds a little panicked.

"Thrust!"

"I don't—"

Whatever protest he was about to make dies when I grind myself backward.

An arm wraps under me, hugging between my breasts and landing near my throat, while he wraps his other around the front of my chest.

Ammos' pelvis *slams* against my butt.

"Yes! Just like that!" I encourage.

He takes over, heaving his breaths into my ear, the sweat collecting on my back sticking to his chest, and because his skin sort of feels like rock, every time it drags over me, it kind of reminds me of being fucked up against a brick wall—*good times*—and the areas where he's roughly textured feel wickedly delicious as they scrape up my skin.

I can really feel a build now. This next one is going to be *fantastic.*

Teeth clamp onto my neck.

It's exactly the right amount of sweet, *sweet* sting and it shocks me into a climax, shaking my arms so hard I can't hold us up anymore—even the backs of my thighs are twitching, *all* of me is twitching—my muscles are seizing so strongly that I'm reminded of the electrified prison batons, but this feels freaking amazing.

It crashes, that heavenly relief from the aftermath pouring through me, and I feel like a limp noodle as I sink myself down as far as I can go, suddenly feeling exhausted.

I'm still hooked to Ammos though.

And now it feels awkward.

He's still panting in my ear, and I've become aware of liquid running down my legs. It feels like I'm in the shower, warm water cascading over me, and this makes me uncomfortable since I'm very clearly not there, and this is very clearly not water pouring out of my insides.

This must be his nectar.

And it's feeding me.

This is *so* weird.

"I can see your body growing health back," Ammos meekly shares.

"That's good." I'm not sure what else to say. "How do you feel?"

The word rushes out of him. *"Amazing."* I feel him tense on top of me. "How are you feeling?"

"Oddly not hungry anymore. And where I'm from, we don't get fed this way, so it's taking some getting used to. But it's nice. I felt like I was starving, I got great O's, and no calories and ta-dah, here we are, best diet ever." I chance a look over my shoulder, and despite our faces' proximity, he manages to hold our eye contact, so I smile.

Tentatively, he smiles back. "I'm going to remove my rootstem from your hollow. Well, not that you're hollow, it is a moist cavern—"

I reach up and pat his hand, which is still resting on my shoulder. "I vote against moist cavern."

His face flushes and I lose his eyes again. "I am sorry, I don't know..."

"It's fine—can I suggest pussy? Or vagina? I'll take love-glove at this point. Meat-wrapper. Hang on, I bet we can ask Ryan what words he knows. I have an idea his vocabulary has no bounds on colorful phrases."

I smile but he doesn't see it. I feel his thickness pull out, followed by hefty finger-*strings* which I succeed in pretending that I am not at all disturbed about, and I sit up and move into his space, and when my fingers ghost up his neck and play with the curve of his ear, he darn near jumps away from my hand.

I bite my lip. "I didn't mean to spook you. Can I touch you?"

He exhales and tries to look in my direction. "I *do* like it when you touch me. I know it doesn't seem—I'm not good at showing it."

Even after the sex, he's so keyed up with nerves. I feel sorry for him. "Will you lie on your back for me?"

His eyes glance off of mine. "If you like."

His muscles are stiff and he looks extremely uncomfortable and a little fearful as he settles down and waits for my move.

I shuffle to him on my knees, not self-conscious until I feel the air hit the parts of me that are wet. We soaked the bed.

His eyes flick down, and he looks...

Ammos looks *proud*. He manages to meet my eyes.

I find my lips tugging up in a half-smile.

His ears pick up and his body relaxes.

I ponder this for a moment before I place my fingers on his chest and gently trail my touch down his abdomen. His thighs tense.

I finally satisfy my curiosity and look between his legs.

I'm not sure what I was expecting.

He did refer to his... *member*... as a rootstem. It starts off very man-root like, but instead of having a head to his cock, there are... I'm not sure what to call them. 'Tubers' sounds mildly horrifying.

More than mildly.

They felt so much more delicious than they actually appear. It *is* a good thing I didn't see them first. These aliens could have laid my options out: 'Take this inside you or die' and I know my first choice would have been death by starvation.

Ammos' tubers are a reddish-black, each one having a glans-like end on the tuber-portion part.

They're glistening, and the ends are dripping a very watery, honey-colored substance.

As I watch, they start to lengthen, sort of like they're peeking out at me.

For some bizarre reason, it makes my lips tip up in reaction. I look to Ammos, and find he's watching *me,* a gratifying sort of anticipatory-infatuation in his gaze, and I find myself asking, "Can I touch it—uh, *them?*"

His adam's apple bobs. "Yes."

"It won't hurt?" I verify.

His eyes go round. "I don't think so."

An honest-to-God giggle escapes me before I can catch it.

In response, he grins. It's tentative, and lopsided, and cute, and he holds my gaze the whole time.

I pat his stomach. "I only wonder because in human men, some of them get really sensitive after they come. Sometimes their penis can't be touched at all afterward."

Instead of putting him at ease, he's back to looking alarmed. "I don't think it will hurt."

"Just tell me and I'll stop," I promise him, biting my lip until my eyes water and my breath leaves me in a little *I-want-to-laugh-so-bad-right-now* shudder.

I run the pad of my finger along the head of one of them, and watch his powerful leg muscles twitch in reaction.

His tubers disappear.

Ammos grunts, and I can't tell if it's good or bad or painful, so I ask him.

"I suppose it's because the nectar is drained. The same as Chor."

I blink at him. "Is *that* why Chor is sick?" I'm stunned. "'Feeding me' takes from you?"

He nods, unworried. "A tribe rotates and keeps their azibo from reaching such a critical level." He lifts his arm, plucking something off of it. "Once you've recovered, and maybe after your Sproutling arrives, you won't require nectar in the extreme. Are you tired, nitesh?" He reaches to my face... and sticks a flower in my hair.

Nitesh. This isn't the first time my translator has heard them call me this, but it's the first time it's supplied, *'heartbeat of the earth.'*

Trying to process everything he just said—and everything we just *did*—I reach up, and toy with the petals.

A flashlight shines in my face. It's coming from his *chest.*

Before I can even cover my eyes, it dims to a gentle beam of green.

His ears fold low, before they slowly prick upward, and with visible effort, his eyes latch onto mine again. "Can I... hold you?"

Inexplicably, my face heats. *This* makes me shy? "That would be nice," I manage, and when he opens his arms, I bury my head under his chin so that *I* don't have to look into *his* eyes.

The concept that—without a way to get home, and no way to re-verse what's been done to me—*this is what we have to do...* it's just as sobering as when Ryan and I were talking.

The aliens could make this situation so much worse. Instead, they've been... *nice.*

Without a way to get home, we'll be raising a baby *with* aliens.

My lips quirk. *Sproutling.*

I don't know how to classify the feeling in my chest when Ammos chuckles softly and says, "It is all well," as he gently strokes my shoulder and back. "This will get easier."

CHAPTER 21

RYAN

I RIPPED THE HALVES of a leaf off of its long stem, and I'm using it to tease the freaky little animal that's rolling around next to me.

"You are playing with your food?" Mace asks.

"Affirmative. Caedon was bored in his cage."

Mace's face gets uglier when he drops that ridiculously squared jaw. "You named a vejo-kaolin?"

I shrug. "My food deserves a kickass name."

Clearly, my food couldn't care less about any of the names I've tossed out so far, but I kinda like how it's fucking with Mace a little so I feel like we've got a winner here. "What do you have against my guy?"

"Not a thing. It's simply that keeping vejo-kaolins can be a challenge."

"Why's that?"

"They're irritable."

"Hm. That so." I'm liking this Caedon better and better already.

Mace shoots me a look. "Luck is with you. We have experience in dealing with them. You could even say some of us develop an understanding from time to time. Even a fondness."

Now it's my turn to shoot him a look. "Not too fucking fond, just so we're clear."

He smirks. And that is so damn unsettling on an alien.

Something slaps against my chest. I look down to find a scrap of leather with little strings. "A cock curtain? I feel so included."

"Oooh, nice loincloth," Preta teases as she steps in the room. Her tone's light, easy—but these eyes. *Wary*. She's got to fuck three aliens if she doesn't want to starve to death, but she's wasting energy she doesn't have on how I'm going to react and how I'll treat her.

I open my arms to her. "Come here, Sol."

Surprise. That's the emotion that flashes across her face, and it guts me. Does it bother me to share her? I'm not happy about it, but I'm not going to sit here and punish her for it either, and I need her to know that. I told her, but obviously, I have to show her.

I think I just did.

She's very, very careful not to jostle my thigh when she joins me. And she's almost in my arms when she squeals, "Aww, you took her out!"

"It's a he," I correct.

"How do you know?" she asks.

We both look to Maceous, who's still standing near the doorway, his arms crossed. He sighs and ambles over, and flips Caedon on his back. "It is a male," he confirms.

"Caedon," I inform her, and unlike the alien, my woman nods because she recognizes cool shit when she hears it. I kiss her.

Clearly not expecting it, she hesitates for a second and I swear to fuck, it feels like I got shot again, and this time right in the chest. I catch her throat, and gently thumb over her pulse. "It's okay, Preta. It's all right, okay?"

She searches my eyes before her lids get alarmingly puffy and she says, "Okay."

"Don't cry," I order her before I move in to kiss her again.

I pull back because I feel like we've got a fucking audience. "You looking for pointers?" I ask the big alien.

His grin reaches his eyes. "Yes."

"Fuck off."

With a disgustingly, impressively deep, rumbling laugh, he does, shutting the door behind him.

When I look back at Preta though, it's to see some of that fear has returned now that we're alone. I stroke the nape of her neck. "Hey. I mean it."

Taking a deep breath, she leans her weight into me, and covers my mouth with hers.

My hand makes its way to her bare stomach, and when she eases back so we can breathe, I drag my stubble across her cheek and nibble on her ear before asking, "How are you feeling? How's Devon doing today?"

She grabs my hand and takes her ear from my mouth so she can stare at me. "Devon? *Devon?* You can't make an executive decision to name our baby!"

I lift a shoulder. "Just did."

"Well," she says, and her eyes have lost that bite of anxiety, and are turning to a pretty shade just this side of irritated. I like it. "At least your name option works for both genders."

I softly glide my hand over her belly. This is... *this is fucking* awesome. I've never really gotten to do this with her before. To celebrate that we're even having a baby. There's always been the fear of getting caught.

The fear of losing it.

I watch her expression turn all sappy. I'm afraid mine's gone that way too, so I fuck with her a bit more. My tone is as obnoxiously superior as I can make it. "It doesn't need to work for both genders. Devon's a boy."

She gets right up in my face when she scoffs. "Oh really! How do you know it's a boy?"

We both look to the doorway where Mace just left.

"I just do."

She huffs. "You're full of it. What if Drogan-Sol is a girl?"

I grab her by the hair and pull her in where I can taste her neck. Sweetest fucking spot on the planet...

I pause.

Apparently, *any* fucking planet.

I drop my nose into the hollow where her shoulder meets her pretty throat, inhaling hard before I lick her skin and test the feel of her with my teeth.

"Ryan? What if she's a girl?"

I nip her harder before laving it away. "That'd be fine, I'd love her like crazy, but it's a boy, so I'll love Devon like crazy."

She's caught between incredulity and laughter. "You don't *know*—"

I catch her face so I can look her in the eye. "I do know I love this baby."

Mollified, she finally nods, and thank fuck, because I can go back to her neck where she lets me lick, and bite, and suck to the awesome sounds of her whimpers.

I've never gotten to do this with her either—the holding and the taking my time. It's nice. Fucking overdue.

"Do I smell?"

I pull up. "Huh?"

Her face is red. "I washed, but..."

Oh. Motherfucking *not* a topic I want to wade into. "No. You smell... it's pretty. Like flowers. And sort of earthy, like that really good humus soil they sell, with all the stuff loaded into it to feed your seedlings."

We both go still, staring into each other's eyes. I clear my throat and try not to grimace. "Yeah, okay. I don't want to think too deep on that, okay?"

She swipes her hand through the air. "Deal."

I throw my arm around her and tug her hard into my side. "You all right?"

She shakes her head. I tense.

"Yeah," she clarifies. "It's just all so nuts. I can't wrap my head around everything."

"You and me both, babe."

My tongue lightly drags a path along her shoulder. I see her eyes close, her neck arches to the side, I grip her hair tight in my fist—and she smiles. Beautiful fucking smile.

I can't be this close and *not* keep from touching her, so I go about showing the other side of her neck attention...

And it becomes really fucking apparent that it's already seen some.

There's a giant-ass bite at the base of her throat. That's *my* spot. This is *my* girl. These are not my teeth impressions.

Not gonna lie—I slobber all over her bruised flesh like it'll wash it away faster, and then I go up high on her throat, and take the top spot, the sensitive place where she loves to be held.

It's mine.

She is MINE.

"Feel better?"

I think she's laughing at me. I don't care. "Affirmative."

"Just as long as everybody's clear on who I belong to, right? You sort of growled, '*MINE*,' kind of right in my ear."

Now I feel like a dick. I kiss her ear. "Sorry."

She wraps her arm around me, forgiveness plain enough in her action. She's so sweet. So is this little tribal bikini thing she's wearing. It's got some sort of crisscross thing going on in front, displaying the tops of her pretty tits, while her bottom half is basically begging to be ripped off with my teeth. And with her midriff on display like this it's distracting as hell and all I want to do is touch it. Touch her. So I do. "Fuck, I want you so bad," I tell her.

"We should stop," she says, almost panting now, and I freeze until I hear the second half of her advice, "—before you get too worked up. I don't want to hurt you."

"I'll be fine, baby, don't worry. I have to have you."

She looks worried anyway, her eyes dark and pretty.

Just going to have to prove it.

"This bed is huge," I tell her as I carefully edge away from where a headboard would normally go, and inch my way until I'm positioned how I want to be, where I want to be, and I don't fuck up my leg doing it.

"What are you doing?" Preta asks, laughter plain in her voice.

I cock an eyebrow as I slowly recline until my head is touching the bed. "Climb on my face and find out."

CHAPTER 22

PRETA

I CAREFULLY CURL INTO his side. "How weird is this?"

Ryan picks up Caedon, peering into the beady yellow eyes. "Scale of one to ten? Undefinable, but we'll deal."

I can feel that my smile is crooked when I blab, "Does it help to know they have a bit of a refractory period?" My muscles tense, afraid I shouldn't have gone here, shouldn't venture near any details about the sex. Now I feel like I sort of have to commit though. "Their 'feeding'... they can only have sex once every few days."

One definitive nod. "That does make me feel better."

Relief. "Really?"

His fingers spear into my hair and he uses this grip to pull me out of my hiding spot at his throat so he can look me in the eyes. "Damn straight. May not be able to 'feed you,'" he finger quotes the air, "but I can be here to satisfy your orgasm quotient for the day."

I move my lips to his neck, and smile into his throat. "Yes, please."

I watch him pluck a hank of fur from his friend, and pop it into his mouth.

Strange. "It's like troll hair," I observe, fascinated, as Ryan takes another bite of Caedon's fur.

"Cotton candy," he either adds or corrects, I can't tell, but I'm weirdly, morbidly captivated watching him munch on it. "It even sort of disintegrates once it mixes with saliva."

"Interesting."

He grimaces. "Geez. Be glad you get magic dick. This 'food' tastes like shit."

I choke a little but try to nod sympathetically. "I'm sorry."

He glances up, his expression losing its irritation at the food, instantly replacing with concern. "I was kidding. Come here," he says as he catches the back of my neck and brings my mouth to his. When he allows me to pull away, it's only far enough that our eyes can focus on the other, and I watch his dance when he breathes against my lips, "Told ya."

His playfulness is so not what I expected—I laugh.

Then I gag.

He grins huge, and lets me go completely. He's having a grand time watching me wipe my lips with the back of my hand. "Ugh, you weren't kidding! That's *awful*."

He nods.

I scrape at my tongue and try to talk at the same time, so my words come out wet and garbled, but I manage. "I can share magic dick with you."

He shudders into his next handful. "No need," he answers easily. "I'll eat my friends, thanks," and to leave no doubt, he scoops up Caedon and drops him on his lap before he tugs me so I'm squished into his side, the spot between my legs still happy and a little beard-burned.

CHAPTER 23

MACEOUS

"DUDE. I'D LIKE IT very much if we could stop hugging like this."

I heave Ryan upward. It isn't that he's heavy; it's that he's unwilling. If he had claws, he'd be digging them into the bed, forcing me to peel him up out of it. I sigh.

"Don't breathe on me."

"Sniveling *spore*," I growl. "Do you want me to carry you up, or would you like to bathe with a pitcher and basin again?"

"Really wish we could have arranged this back when I was still wearing pants."

Preta, who is keeping an apprehensive watch beside me, reaches up and pats him on the stomach. "For what it's worth, you look pretty hot in a loincloth."

He points to her, then to me, his finger nearly stabbing me in the face. "*Exactly* what I'm afraid of."

Preta laughs, and I take full note of Ryan's transformation; he relaxes, he falls silent, and the smile that spreads across his face is sardonic, and pleased.

I grumble about being grafted to husbandmen with such a choleric disposition all through the tunnels—and I thank sunshine for females.

Once we've exited the hometree, I shift to my Guardian form, and Preta's obvious awe at seeing this causes a proud coil of amusement to bloom inside me.

"Here," Ammos says, edging up to me, already Shifted. I place Ryan on Ammos' back and despite Ryan's curse-laden complaining about being shuttled to 'yet another lizard,' he seems rather pleased with his new station high above the ground.

He reminds me much of my older brother, who was the cantankerous husbandman in his group of husbandmen.

It seems there's a sour one in every pod; I assumed I'd fill the role.

How was I to know ours would in fact have *two*.

I feel the row of scales that cover my upper lip pull tautly upward at the corners.

Ryan glances at me before complaining, "Mom, tell the dragon it's creepy when he smiles."

Preta's arms contort as she skids to a halt. Her lip curls in horror. "Eww."

Ryan throws back his head, and the laughter that erupts from his throat sounds more like a bark.

She is busy sending him a look of mock disapproval, so she is startled when Chor takes her hand. He guides her to stand at the area just behind my shoulder, where he boosts her onto my back before he clambers up himself. He's nearly at full strength again, but there's no need to tax him when I can easily be responsible for the journey.

"How is your leg?" Preta calls to Ryan, her tone full of concern.

"Dunno. Might have been a little accidental brilliance to do this after all; stretches it without bearing weight."

"Yeah?"

He shrugs. "I've no fucking clue, actually," he admits. He grins at her, and I feel her knees squeeze my sides. "But I prefer to do the riding up top than be the one getting cuddled between his hands."

"Stop it," she sounds like she's covering her face, but her voice holds mirth. "They're trying to help you. Play nice."

"You—

Ammos' snort cuts off their banter, and flower petals float down to the ground as he shakes his head at them. He takes lead, pulling ahead of me.

I hear Preta's surprised, "We're not flying?"

I turn my head enough so that I can see her while keeping a side-view of the path ahead. "It'd likely be too taxing on Ryan's leg," I explain. "Until he's strong enough to use it to help him stay upright and on during flight, this way will be the smoothest mode of travel. There is also the benefit of you both having the chance to see more of your new home."

"Oh, thank you! Very thoughtful—and appreciated," she adds. She is quiet a moment. "What's in the bag?"

Since I carry no bag, I know she's got her attention on Chor. I can smell tar soap, and I imagine he's been using his recuperation period to make it for her.

In Guardian form, we've not had need of soap. I'm impressed he remembered how to create it.

I watch when he gifts it to her; she's surprised, and touched, and I find I'm pleased by extension.

This is an interesting development. Her happiness, our accomplishments to that end; we'll all feel the effects.

I'm especially impressed at how Petrichor appropriated her presence so smoothly—I'm not certain if his guiding her towards us, rather than putting her with Ryan, was intentional. But as Chor stays unnaturally quiet, I'm starting to believe he's giving me time with her, and offering her a chance to grow comfortable with me.

I am simply at a loss on what to say to put her at ease.

"Beautiful garden."

Thank sunshine. I heave a massive sigh of relief, and feel four knees adjust their grip on me.

I stop walking, and see that Ammos halts too, close enough that Ryan can hear also. "This is Geoss. Over there is Micha, and that is Dikar, Granith, Prakrti, and then Adarian—

"You name your gardens?"

My back dips when I twist my neck enough to fully face her. "Our people all have names."

I'm not surprised she shows no comprehension. The Kahav are a tribe tied to the earth; her people are different—she's never encountered the like in her own tribe. I look to Geoss again, seeing what she must see: flowers on a hill, gracefully growing in a line. They follow a path along his form, and I know when she sees that they make his Guardian shape because she rears back, blinking in shock. I nod at her. "These are our people when they go to earth."

It's clear she doesn't only find the sight beautiful: she finds it sad. "What happened to your people?"

I drag my snout back and forth against my shoulder. "When the Ruler arrived, we worked. There's a city of ruins not far from here—it was a great place once. It was nearly completed when blight came. Our females succumbed quickly, and their husbandman followed."

She leans forward, stretching out her fingers, but can't reach me. After a moment, I press my snout to the underside of her hand, and she drags her nails up and down in just the right spot. "Where is your Ruler now?"

Sighing with relief, I straighten and start off again, forcing Ammos to move forward. "His workforce was gone. He abandoned the survivors too young to be of any good to him. He's never returned."

Ryan looks at me over his shoulder. "You're unbelievably chill about being exploited."

I shrug, which makes Preta curse with a laugh and catch the bases of my wings in order to keep her seat. She's in no danger of falling; Chor would never let that happen, and I imagine he just wrapped his arm around her, because Ryan's expression moves to a resolved sort of acceptance.

He's trying. When he looks back at me, I incline my head. "We've had lifetimes to understand we can't change it. It's simple: rail at the unfairness, or move on."

I feel Preta's hand stroke softly between my shoulders.

CHAPTER 24

PRETA

IT'S SIMPLE: RAIL AT the unfairness, or move on.

Staring through water so clear I can see to the bottom, to a rainbow of color like I've never seen before; it feels possible to accept everything that's happened—and to move on from it. Everything right *here* is peaceful. Right here, it feels like this is all that really matters.

I've got a baby to raise, and the makings for a strange-but-awesome family for this baby.

I've got to thank the programming; I'm not completely useless with grief over *my* family. I worry about them, but it's like it's being monitored and kept at a controlled level.

Charlie's safe. Dad's fine. I feel it. Carry on.

I could be wrecked over this, but at some point I have to choose to find the happy. Maybe this is my programming talking, but I feel like I can have it here if I try. Right now, it doesn't feel as if it will be hard.

I scrubbed like a madwoman the moment I was submerged, and now I've been soaking, just enjoying the... peace.

The guys are all lounging—on rocks, in the water, and out of it, and they're giving each other crap, and soaking up the sun, and Ryan's even laughing with them, shooting the breeze, comfortable with their presence.

Relaxed looks good on him.

Happy looks good on him.

It all feels good on me.

I drag my hand over the rocks below me. It's not that 'this rock looks sort of pink,' or 'this one kind of greenish'—no, they're inspired-by-crayons *bright* shocks of unreal colors, making this lake possibly the most incredible thing I've ever seen.

And I've seen dragons made out of trees. My bar's kind of high.

Speaking of dragons, it's a good thing our baby is going to grow up around them and live in a great big hobbit-tree because little Drogan-Sol is going to need all the help she can get. When we arrived at the shore, I said it looked like a rainbow had broken into pieces and rained down, and Ryan stubbornly refused to get excited about it. He was all, "Water droplets in the atmosphere that catch sunlight and refract aren't going to 'break into pieces' and turn into rocks, babe. Sorry."

I'd clutched my stomach, talking over him, and offering advice right to the occupant of my womb. "Ignore him. You're going to be amazingly creative. Somehow, you will not inherit his anti-imagination gene. Mostly because there can't be two of you. There can't be!"

"Is this about the cloud gazing?"

"This is totally about the cloud gazing! You won't watch the clouds with me; I've got to raise somebody who will."

He caught me and pulled me into his chest. "I'll watch *you*."

"Awww," I'd started to say, melting.

His breath warm on my face as he looked down at me, he'd promised, "I'll gaze on you while you watch the collected moisture—"

I'd thrown my hands up between us, shoving at him. "Ugh! Stop! You're *terrible*."

Even now, I'm still shaking my head at him, and every time he catches me, he's still laughing.

I purse my lips at him, and pull my tongue away from my upper palate to make that disgusted little *tsk!* noise. Sad. Just sad.

Secretly though, I'm loving the sound of Ryan's laughter. Petri-chor's too. They're each on partially submerged slabs of rock, done bathing and they genuinely seem to be enjoying each other's company.

It makes my brain happy.

It makes my programming happy too.

My stomach however, is not happy. It's growling, and I'm getting nervous butterflies, because I've hit upon the realization that the hungrier I am, the more it drains my... husbandmen.

One day, I might be able to say that word and not blink. A lot.

For now, I shake off the weirdness trying to settle over me. Talking with Mace today eased my anxiety quite a bit. Instead of having him watch me quietly suffer, all while knowing that he's going to pay for it after, I need to start taking the initiative. Pep talk taking effect enough to embolden me, I press through the hip-high water, and make my approach.

Ryan seems to have spied something, and when I delay a second in order to see what's caught his attention—an odd sort of calcified-formation—he sputters, "Those look like... wellheads... turbine... and is that a condenser? What the...! Earth power. '*Earth* power!' You guys have geothermal power sources? You treat gunshot wounds with decaying vegetation but you have *geothermal power?* Are you kidding me?"

CHAPTER 25

MACEOUS

CHOR WEARS A SLY GRIN, but he sobers it to a mock-offended expression. "What? Did you think we were a band of jungle savages?"

"YES."

I chuckle along with them, appreciating this camaraderie, enjoying the sun heating my moss. With direct light this strong, I don't feel it growing at the moment.

When Ryan's eyes drop from mine, I look down too, and find *Preta*—looking up at *me*.

I'm not surprised; the Sproutling has been getting louder and louder in its tiny demands. "Ready?" I ask her.

"You make me nervous," is her reply. Her eyes go round and the water laps around her as she stiffens. "I didn't mean to say that out loud, but there you go. I... need nectar. Would you like to be the one to... do you want to have sex?"

My smile is slow, but genuine, especially as her facial color intensifies. "I would like this very much. Thank you for inviting me."

She skims the water's surface with her hand. "Yeah, nothing in life has prepared me for this conversation. I feel like I'm the one that should be thanking you for feeding me with your... Where should we do this?"

Slowly, I bring my hand up to press her hair back. She was watching the water though, not me, so it startles her. She recovers quickly, even bringing her hand up, bumping into mine before I take hold of it and guide it to trace over the flower I just placed behind her ear.

This one has been growing on my chest since Ryan blooded me. I've been waiting for the right moment to gift it to her, and my heartstone glows brightly when she smiles.

I glance at Ryan. His gaze is on my hand, where it has taken Preta's, and he's lost most of his easy joviality.

He doesn't appear angered, or saddened though. *Accepting.* He appears accepting. And when his eyes meet mine, one side of his mouth kicks upward. "I'm onto your flower secret. Friggin' overachievers," he calls.

He teases. My heartstone flares, and Chor says something that makes Ryan good-naturedly slap water towards his face, and a subtle tension steals out of Preta's shoulders.

I squeeze her hand lightly, and get her smile in return.

Setting off, I lead Preta behind the waterfall she was exploring earlier with Ammos. Though the water isn't rushing hard, it makes enough noise and is moving at enough of a volume that we'll have privacy here.

The water level in this spot is higher—mid-level on me, but on her, the swells of her breasts just tease the surface and are proving quite distracting.

I wait patiently for her to reach for me, but she does not.

I regard her in silence, thinking that it will allow her to collect her thoughts.

What it does, is unnerve her.

Her gentle boldness from before has fled somewhere, and I don't know what I've done to chase it off, nor do I know how to coax it back. Ammos has been deferential and downright docile where she is concerned. I imagine Chor is much the same.

There is nothing submissive about me, but judging from the interactions I've observed when she is with Ryan, I don't believe Preta minds. Yet she is uncomfortable, pulling further away from me, taking great interest in the tiny cavern we stand in, examining the curtain of water that gives us this haven.

It must be something about me; she's clearly struggling with how best to proceed with *me*.

I don't ask her if she'd rather have me approach. I just do.

One step in her direction has me towering over her. Her lips part, a silent breath escaping, and her beautiful eyes, nearly the same shade as the tender insides of a mehyam nut, lock with mine.

The sound of the water breaking as I bring my hand up to cup her face has her jerking, but she settles, and from the side, I execute a stealth touch, skimming my palm along the comely curve of her hip. When I lean in to catch her lips, her eyes go hooded.

I slide my hand to her mound.

A tap of prevernal pollen has her gasping into my mouth, latching onto my shoulders, buoying herself in the water so that she can scramble up my body.

Her lower covering is rucked up between us, so it is nothing to knead the luscious handfuls of her rumpflesh. I caress her smooth back, sighing against her cheek when I pull away from her mouth to breathe.

I am ready to bury my rootstem inside of her, but she's grown curious about my chest vines so I exercise patience as she lifts a hand from the water and presses a dripping fingertip to my dry areas, seemingly fascinated by my skin's reaction as it absorbs the dampness and sprouts a small leaf.

"Like marl!" she says.

I don't know what that means, but it's distracting to know that her Sproutling is hungry, starting to loudly crave tapriklut again—while I'm consumed with a need of a very different sort; I feel my tendrils swelling to a painful degree, and if we don't hurry, I'm fearing they'll have grown too big to all fit inside of her.

While she satisfies her curiosity, I start at her chin, just under her slightly kiss-swollen lip, trailing soft presses and licks down her jaw, making my way to her throat where I see someone has already marked her neck.

Not to be outdone, I nip it, my teeth going between the top bite, and the bottom bite.

She cries out, her lower half bucking against me, before she suddenly seizes, her limbs going rigid, her toes curling into my calves.

The moment it breaks, I crowd her opening, driving my rootstem forward, attempting to stuff my thickened tendrils past her bizarrely wonderful, tight ring of inner muscle.

"Ahhh!" she cries, and I go still, but before I can panic that I've hurt her, I *sense* her enjoyment.

I groan with gratitude. I am relieved I do not have to stop. She feels... her slick, inner heat rivals *magma*.

I feel my tendrils disperse, feel them inspecting her insides, and when one taps her upper wall, I feel pleasure accumulate in my pelvic region, so intense I feel like I'm bursting.

Her body is calling my nectar. She draws it from me, and I'm grateful the water is helping to keep us upright, and failing that, at least we'll have a gentle landing.

I stagger backward, crashing against the cavern wall.

She doesn't even notice.

She's writhing on me, riding my stem, *moving* on me.

When she grinds us together, and her insides squeeze from the base of my rootstem to the tips of my fanned out tendrils, I rumble with shocked approval. "Preta..."

She moves her hands from my shoulders, and wraps them around my neck, clinging to me, our chests pressed together, the scent of crushed flowers and leaves and vines wafting up between us.

My doublethumbs catch at the fetching hollows at the base of her spine. She arches her back, her head coming up, her mouth finding my ear as she pants, "You don't normally *move*, do you?"

I pull back far enough to take note of her life-flushed face, her darkened eyes, the dew gathered on her skin that is causing the hair at her temples to stick. "Not naturally. A Kahav female has a fertile hollow for us to bury tendrils. We twine together, and the male half supplies nectar, and seed."

Her question excites me, and I grope her until I find I can clasp her hips and use them to lift her and recreate her grinding motion, but on a much, *much* pleasanter scale.

She gasps in my ear, I grunt, and I yank her up this time, and slam her down on my stem.

My tendrils thrash wildly and she squeezes my neck hard before she starts mindlessly kissing the side of my face.

I drag her up, and repeat.

Faster.

Harder.

She's squeaking with every downward drag, and my nectar releases in a forceful pulse when I thrust up into her.

She digs her chin into my shoulder, my hands have to be bruising her soft skin as I drag her body along my shaft and yank her down, until her inner tension releases in bursts, her body shaking, her insides flattening my tendrils as they squeeze every last drop of nectar from me.

I bellow, "Drogan!"

Startled, Preta begins to pull herself up but I keep her clamped tightly to me, nuzzling the spot on her neck that I marked, and quickly, she relaxes back into my embrace.

From behind the waterfall, Ryan hollers, "DON'T SAY MY NAME WHEN YOU NUT. IT'S FUCKING WEIRD."

CHAPTER 26

PRETA

IT'S 'TARN TIME!' Over the last, oh, two weeks, three?—Chor, Mace, and Ammos have taken us to a new tarn each outing. They're staggered one over the other, climbing in elevation as far as the eye can see.

It makes for a gorgeous view when we've gone up high, and peered over the edge, seeing them all laid out below us, a riot of colors and crystalline perfection.

We didn't go up high today, because Ryan *walked here on his own two feet*. He's limping like a sonofagun, but he's *made* it, and I know I can't baby him, and he'd hate it if I tried.

I worry my bottom lip as I watch him go right for the water, and I hear him hiss, "Thank dead veggies."

He looks back at me, so I know he was trying to make me laugh. When he sees I can't, his strained expression softens. "Get in here."

I do, and he squeezes me, drags his stubble over the top of my head, giving me a moment to collect myself before he says, "I'm fine. It just got hot."

Before I can do more than stiffen, he's quick to assure me. "No infection: chill." He gives me a tighter squeeze. "Just getting used to being worked again. 'Kay?"

Hugging him back, I nod under his chin.

"All right. Go frolic with your dragons." He gives me a tiny ill-behaved shove.

See? He won't let me baby him.

When he catches me watching him scratch at his jaw, he growls, "Preta."

I'm not worrying over him now as much as I'm remembering this morning when he shaved.

Ryan was very much grateful to find out our aliens have razor blades.

The guys have razor blades because they 'trim the moss' off their faces.

Every morning, I watch them in fascination. In different *kinds* of fascination. I grin as I watch Ryan because it's hot to see a man shave.

I smile in bewilderment watching my tree-dragons because I'm equal parts horrified that living organisms have to be shorn off their jaws and chin, yet at the same time, I enjoy ogling the way their back muscles move and the way a loin cloth doesn't cover all of their ass.

I'm pregnant. Not dead.

I jump them just about every time. We have to schedule who I watch in the morning so that I don't attack any one of them too often.

It's insane.

I sigh happily, and Ryan smirks at me a second before he squeezes a fistful of water and it jets into my face.

"Jerk!" I squeal, but I'm laughing.

Charlie.

I pause. I've got goosebumps all of a sudden.

Charlie.

I take a deep breath. I tell myself that Charlie is fine. I don't know how I know it, but I do feel that she's fine. It's the same feeling I have about Lydia, Zoya, Quinn and Yahiro from the Alpha pod trials.

How do I know this? How *could* I know this?

I'd asked Ryan about it. "But *how* do I know?"

I've squished those spotted beetles, the ones that swarm, and when they sense that one of their own is harmed, the infestation riles up, squirting nasty stuff and pinching everything they feel threatened by.

I wondered what else the research team added to me. This isn't just me trying to reassure myself. Somehow, *I feel people I care about.*

Ryan's jaw muscle had started twitching like he was reliving memories he'd rather not. "Whatever else they did to you was above my pay grade."

Like he said before, he was a grunt and they considered him no more than living furniture. Dumb but mostly useful. Talking around him was fine, but it wasn't like they'd ever have sat down chatted with him about how it all worked.

Guards were there to watch, not think.

I sigh now, and rub a hand over my arm, trying to get the hairs to lay flat.

Charlie!

She's so front and center in my mind, that for a second, I think my head is playing tricks on me when I see her in the water below us.

It's the four hulking *finned* creatures circling her that tip me off.

Unless sister mirages come with some sort of aquatic aliens, *that's my sister down there* for real!

"CHARLIE!" The sound of the water splashing is totally drowning out my voice as I try to run to the shore. I see my guys, every one of them, look up sharply as I shriek. I don't wait for them—I run past them like a crazy person. "Charlie!"

Charlie slams into me, and we're hugging, and I'm spazzing on her, and then she's yanking away from me, shocked.

Last time she saw me, I looked like one of those underfed underwear models.

After they get addicted to heroin.

We're in the middle of loudly reuniting, when I hear Mace. Not his speaking voice; his *dragon's* bellow.

He goes full Apatosaurus, *smashing* his tail into the new alien standing closest to me, sending him sailing into the air!

Suddenly, the clear sky turns, and we're standing in the middle of a terrifying mini-tsunami, leaves and vines whipping—

Oh no. The vines aren't being torn up by wind; they're shooting from *my* aliens! They're headed for *Charlie's* aliens!

A wave of water comes at us, but just as I'm preparing to watch us all drown, it lands... around us. We're not touched.

Relieved, gasping, I look up to see that Ammos has joined Mace, hell-bent on colliding with the alien Mace lashed, and as one of Charlie's guys checks that she's okay, from behind me, I sense Petrichor.

He snarls, so deep that the vibration of it skitters up my back.

Chor?

Heart hammering, I spin and shout at him—at all of them. "Stop!"

Chapter 27

I HAVE AMAZING ALIENS.

The fighting stopped immediately.

And then Mace brought the earth up to trip Charlie's alien and a water jet nailed Ammos in the eye and then it was Charlie shouting for everyone to calm their shit down, and Ryan pointed out they could do that if Charlie's aliens weren't being dicks and while I appreciate that he jumped to their defense...

Charlie's gone dead still.

In that moment, I know exactly what she sees with his 'military-issue' buzz cut, and I know exactly what scenarios she's imagining as she prowls towards him.

It takes some fast talk to assure her that my guard didn't take any advantage of me that I didn't want him to while I was in prison—or out of it!—and it takes some good natured teasing to get her relaxed, but whew, my heart leaps with joy when I catch her up on the big news—and she catches me up on hers.

We're *both* gonna have 'Sproutlings!'

I'm ready to clap my hands and grab her arms and jump up and down, so relieved to have my sister safe, to have her *here,* and I'm so excited that I get to be aunt, and—

Wait.

I look at her aliens. Her fishy-aliens. Fins, gills, alien-eyes, alien hands—

My eyes drop down, wondering just what, uh, what *her* aliens are packing. Thankfully, they're wearing pants because I'm pretty sure it's rude to ogle your sister's alien's junk—but man, I'm curious.

I'm suddenly curious about a lot of things. She's human. They're basically a legged male, mermaid! "But how?"

"What do you mean how? Same as you."

I very, very much doubt that.

"Valos," she finishes confidently.

I look at my aliens. Ummm... *Hide, Ryan!* "This baby isn't valo." My hand goes to my stomach, and instinctively, my eyes dart to Ryan.

The air charges proportionally to the length of silence that stretches out from these words to her outburst.

"You *fucked* a guard!"

See? I knew she wasn't going to take this well.

"The guard has a name, and I'm right here," Ryan bitches.

I roll my lips before clearing my throat. "His name is Ryan." I want to smile at him, because we're all going to be able to laugh about this someday. Charlie will come around—

"You fucked a guard *willingly?*"

Okay, so right now, she's a little horrified, but she'll be okay! She just needs a chance to get to know Ryan.

Charlie dives for him.

Blink. I've got her arm. My mouth is opening to order everyone to move, when I hear Drogan's words from when my programming was just starting to get hacked and overtaken by my pregnancy drives: *'It initiated like a protect-mode, and you want to move your unit away from the threat.'*

Charlie's no threat. Rational me *knows* this; I consciously relax, and I can even joke to myself that I caught her just in time—I saw what she did to *her* guard—I happen to like *my* guard's pretty face, and Charlie's got that mean elbow.

My extreme reaction has me making a note to fill my sister in on the fact that there are phrases she can never say around me. She's going to have to talk to Ryan in order to find out what these even are.

I shake her to get her attention. I'm marveling though: she's awful impressive, with this instantaneous killer haze. Hers is borne of equal parts training and sisterly (over)protectiveness, not laboratory-infused, but all the same, it is awe-inspiringly *fierce!*

Still. She *knows* I'm a big girl. She knows I wouldn't be playing Swiss Family Robinson if I'd spaceship wrecked with a creeper guard. I'm not stupid!

I narrow my eyes at her. I *love* her, but I'm growing a little freaking offended here!

Taking one look at my face, Charlie laughs.

And just like that, we're okay. She pulls me in for a hug, and everyone relaxes.

Note to self: maybe wait to inform Charlie of my *Care-of-Concord* gifts... the ones that altered my nutritional needs. Since she's got her own aliens, I'm pretty sure she'll laugh over how we've been making do here, not freak, but she will *not* like hearing what the research team did to me.

I mean, look how she reacted when she thought I'd been forced by a prison guard!

No need to give her a heart attack within the first five minutes of being reunited.

I rub the back of my neck and send her a grin.

That surprise can wait until supper time.

EPILOGUE

PETRICHOR

THE OTHER EVENING, a strong storm shook the hometree straight to its roots, and silt dropped into our mugs of freshly brewed zemerac tea. All three members of the human tribe reacted somewhat poorly.

"Stop this incessant whining!" Maceous ordered. "It is just dirt."

Charlie, who had been discussing future housing site options, had looked to her aliens. "Maybe not under a tree."

Today, Preta and her sibling have been aerially inspecting the territories in search of many things, one of them being locations for Charlie's tribe to explore. But the sisters have a greater goal. They say mechanical parts from the ship that brought them can act as a conductor, and allow them the ability to speak with their father on the other side of the stars.

Outrageous.

Yet it makes them happy. Ammos formed a vine for Charlie to hold onto, and she described an Earthen method of clamping a rider's feet to a mount's sides. He repeated the same for Dason, one of Charlie's husbandmen, who sits behind her. Though their mounts don't sound like Kahav Guardians, the trick is working and I have rigged Preta in the same.

Mace swoops past us, Ryan pressed low along his back to reduce air resistance in his quest for speed. "Keep up, *Grandpa*," he quips, returning the mystifying insult that Dason lobbed at him earlier.

The humans have a competitive spirit that encourages us to race each other for the simple enjoyment of listening to them playfully trade these boasts and insults.

This scent...

My nostrils flare, and I feel Preta's knees tighten as my ribcage spreads with my great inhale.

"What is it?" Preta shouts over the air current.

This... seems almost familiar.

There's no need to signal the others; Mace and Ammos have caught it too. We make our way down, darting below the canopy and landing gently, ever-mindful of our precious cargo.

I look to Ryan, and feel my lips lift above my fangs, air cooling my gums.

"Quit it," he orders without heat.

Like it or not, he too is precious cargo. Even if he does find our Guardian-form smiles disturbing.

There is no need for the humans to dismount; as soon as we three Kahav touch soil, we find the source of the scent. It is a dead being.

A dead human being.

It smells faintly like Preta and Charlie, but not Ryan, and I suppose this is because the corpse is female.

It appears there was a great struggle. This is not so very surprising; every time we have come upon humans, there is some sort of altercation. They do not seem to be the most peaceful of species.

I look to our humans, curious to their reaction at seeing yet another of their kind fallen, but their expressions are devoid of anything but wariness.

Kahav have excellent vision, and it is Ammos that drops his head, nudging his nose across the shine amongst the dirt. When he uncovers it enough, he catches it in his teeth, and twists his neck to place the find in Charlie's small palm.

Charlie peers down at the thing, and her lash-fronds wave rapidly as she blinks in clear consternation. "Preta?"

"Yeah?" Preta's legs squeeze my sides and I feel her rump leave my back as she stands in the stirrup-contraption and peers at her sibling's hand.

"Preta, this is *my* dog tag."

I feel Preta's jolt of surprise as she half-shouts, "No way!" She pauses. "The prison let you keep your tags? I don't remember seeing them when we got to hug at the crash site."

Charlie's brow turfs have climbed high on her head. "Nope. I knew they'd be confiscated as soon as I got to the prison, so I took them off. I left them with Dad."

Now it is my turn to startle as Preta *falls* into the riding position. Then, the sisters begin *shrieking*.

It is as completely disturbing as it was the first time it occurred.

We are always on guard against threats, but a creature would have to be mad to approach anything making this sort of clamor.

Ammos' ears are laid back flat as he watches the siblings communicate, and Mace is shaking his head along with Ryan, and I am—despite the shrillness to their din—enjoying the liveliness in their exchange. Life had been too quiet before the humans arrived. Life had gone... dormant. The humans have changed everything.

They've given us a tribe again.

They've given us a place to belong.

They're beginning to wind down enough that I can finally understand actual words in their echolocations. Preta half-sonars, "*HERE? DAD IS HERE?*"

This encourages even Ryan to join in, though his voice lacks the extreme pitch the siblings can manage.

A feeling akin to liquid sunshine curls around my heartstone as I listen to them converse, and theorize. *Humans make life interesting.*

I twine a vine up my azibo's—*my nitesh's*—torso, flowers blooming as I snuggly weave an excited Preta in a loving embrace. *They make life worth living.*

Printed in Great Britain
by Amazon